BOTTLE
ROCKET
HEARTS

BOTTLE
ROCKET
HEARTS

A NOVEL BY

ZOE WHITTALL

Cormorant Books

Canada Council
for the Arts
Conseil des Arts
du Canada

The publisher gratefully acknowledges the support of the
Canada Council for the Arts and the Ontario Arts Council
for its publishing program. We acknowledge the financial support
of the Government of Canada through the Book Publishing
Industry Development Program (BPIDP) for our publishing activities.

Printed and bound in Canada

National Library of Canada Cataloguing in Publication

Whittall, Zoe
Bottle rocket hearts / Zoe Whittall.

ISBN 978-1-897151-06-8

1. Title.

PS8595.H4975B68 2007   C813'.6   C2007-900419-9

Cover design: Angel Guerra/Archetype
Text design: Tannice Goddard/Soul Oasis Networking
Cover image: Andrew Holbrooke/Corbis
Editor: Marc Côté
Printer: Transcontinental

CORMORANT BOOKS INC.
215 SPADINA AVENUE, STUDIO 230, TORONTO, ONTARIO, CANADA M5T 2C7
www.cormorantbooks.com

 Mixed Sources
Product group from well-managed
forests, controlled sources and
recycled wood or fiber
www.fsc.org Cert no. SW-COC-000952
© 1996 Forest Stewardship Council
FSC

for all the tough girls I have loved

Especially
Ruth Mary Whittall, 1910–2004,
who was definitely one tough lady.

"I would like to fall in love again but my only hope is that love doesn't happen to me so often after this. I don't want to get so used to falling in love that I get curious to experience something more extreme — whatever that might be."

— DOUGLAS COUPLAND, FROM *LIFE AFTER GOD*

1

COLD, COLD HEARTS

Montreal General Hospital waiting room
December 1996

A fluid that tastes like floor cleaner is dripping down the back of my throat. I'm jittery. Seven is more jittery, and he's making the other people in the waiting room uncomfortable. We are waiting for Della, who's locked up somewhere inside the hospital. We are not family. We're waiting on faith that eventually we'll be allowed to see her. This is somewhat ironic because we've been avoiding her for a number of weeks; her pessimism and anxiety had been like a cheese-grater across our hopeful faces. We are bothering the nurse at the front desk, but we don't mean to. We hold hands, kids scared of what we don't know.

I have a notebook open in my lap. Seven is trying to read over my shoulder. *In this liminal space, we are marking the hospital chairs with dirt-filled, creased spiral marks from the pads of our fingers.* That's the only sentence I have written so far, my pen pressed hard into the thin lined paper, each letter perfectly formed. There is so much dirt married to both of my hands it's hard to imagine wanting it washed off. It's coffee grinds and compost, dirt from the café floor where I fell palms down an hour ago. The silent vows exchanged between the dirt and sterile whiteness are more committed than anything I've known recently.

"Go get us coffee from the vending machine." Direct orders are best, considering Seven's probable state of mind, a June bug bouncing against a light bulb, the bulb being the world outside his body. He stands up as if I wound up a giant key in his back. He walks with a purposeful sashay to the end of the hall. I pick at the dried-up muffin mix stuck to my apron.

Rachel wrote everything she ever thought down on paper. Not just the poetry she lived for, but the mechanical details of her emotional day-to-day. When she was sad she'd write: *I am sad today*, and it somehow transformed her. "*I'm always exercising the tools,*" she'd say, when I'd find her hunched over her notebooks at the kitchen table at 4:00 a.m.

When Rachel's parents went through her room after she died, they found journals from as far back as 1978. Since her death, I've been journaling like mad. I haven't kept a diary since grade seven, and that was really just a list of dates I wanted to have with Jordan from New Kids on the Block. People who journal always seem a little more grounded.

I could use some perspective.

When Rachel experienced a creative block she wrote simple lists on paper torn from a notepad fixed to a fridge magnet. Illustrated cats paraded joyfully around its border, one curled asleep atop the text *shopping list* written in a fancy font at the top. It was likely a gift from her mother, who was prone to mailing Rachel packages that included clippings from the *Sherbrooke Record* announcing the upcoming nuptials of former classmates, flowery homemade items from the county fair, tea cozies, mugs with puppies on them and Jesus-centric items she'd immediately throw away, until Seven began collecting Jesus items. We now have a Jesus wall in the living room with floor-to-ceiling saviour kitsch, with peel-off holographic stickers of his likeness and fluorescent postcard crucifixion scenes.

The notepad looked out of place against our kitchen, painted the colour of a stomach lining, the black and white checkered floor, the framed tattered poster of a pink triangle that reads *Silence = Death*. Every once in a while Seven takes the poster down and says it's out of date, that Act-Up is over and Queer Nation is dead. Then he puts it up again when he gets nostalgic.

I would find Rachel's lists on the table under take-out menus and phone bills. *Some notes on me right now* is how most of them would start. "It grounds me," she'd explain before shyly ripping the paper from my hands, blushing.

I turn to a new page in my journal. *Some notes on me right now: I don't remember what my natural hair colour is. I'm about to turn twenty-one. I just lost my job about an hour ago. I'm losing Della too, but nothing is certain, really.*

And no one ever really has each other. That's the problem right? When you feel entitled to another person. That's more dangerous than jumping out of a plane.

I always used to feel like a pink layer cake or a shoelace trailing that won't ever stay tied. I'm too aloof. Eve does not live up to her potential, says every cardboard report card from high school. I am an only child. I am hard to get to know. Everyone says that. People assume I'm more complicated than I am. My mascara always runs, not in rivers but highways paved down my citied face. I hate it when people put their bus transfers in their mouth because they're carrying too much stuff, or file their nails on the Metro. I like it when you order a small coffee to go, and the cup is so small you feel like a Charmkin. Remember those fingernail sized dolls popular in the eighties? I hate it when activists get indignant about not having a television, as if the revolution depends on our inability to remember or care about who shot JR. I have never been off this continent and I've always lived in Quebec. Still, Quebec feels like my estranged cousin. I learned everything I know about sex from Degrassi Junior High *which I watched in badly dubbed French on a black and white TV that only got one channel. My parents didn't believe in cable.*

Maybe my boss will hire me back if I explain. Except explaining would be harder than getting another job. How do you explain throwing a telephone in the face of a hungry hippie girl, who only wanted soup?

Seven returns with two white cups of coffee. It tastes like hot liquefied crackers and old cereal milk. He drinks his like it's Gatorade after a long race, like his throat doesn't care about hot or cold or pain, only liquid. He leans his small white blond head against my shoulder and closes his eyes. He cups his hands together; I notice his tattoo has healed completely. Across his wrist is written in typewriter font: *Rachel, 1971–1996.* It matches my own.

When I graduated from grade six I won an award for best overall academic achievement. I stood on the creaky stage of St. Mary's elementary school in my peach leather Au-Coton belt cinched around my non-ironic acid-washed jean minidress. It came as a shudder-snap revelation: I was a fake. I'd somehow achieved success without really ever trying. I'd come to the conclusion that conventional success and intelligence really didn't mean all that much. Because there I was, winning the highest honour, and all I'd thought about for months was whether Billy St-Cyr would dance with me to "Never Tear Us Apart" by INXS at the Goodbye Elementary noon-hour dance and lip-synch show.

   I've been in love once.

   I close the notebook and walk up to the nurses' station, ask again about Della. The nurse wears half-circle pink earrings, has clumps of aqua eyeshadow in the crease of her eyes, and is evasive in her most communicative moments. She looks at me like I should be a patient. Her eyes may as well reflect tiny TV screens with closed-captioning, a rolling font that reads, *You're one step away from your inevitable straightjacket destiny.* Or maybe this is paranoia from the drugs last night. Maybe I should sit back down, sit straight, feign patience, lock my ankles together gracefully the way my grandmother unsuccessfully tried to teach me to do as a child. At eight years of age I swore I'd die a painful death before anyone forced me into a dress. And look at me know, diamond stud in my nose, red painted toes, a careful peroxide regime, closet full of things that barely cover the "great ass God gave me," according to my aunt Bev, who frequently comments on my physical attributes with a mix of praise and annoyance.

I doodle a page full of stars and hearts around *I've been in love once*. Seven stirs. I turn the page and write *I'm still in love?*

When I think about how to explain love, I think of a cat I had growing up. Her name was Whitey. I named her. I know, I wasn't a particularly imaginative child. She was full-grown when I was five and died on my eighteenth birthday. She used to catch mice in the backyard and eat them, but she would extract the heart with the precision of a dedicated surgeon. She'd leave the hollow muscular organ on my pillow licked clean, or on the flat toe of my black rubber rain boots by the porch door. She would meow in a particularly high pitch, urgently, to alert my attention to the gift. Now that's devotion. How anyone could live up to this in a human body is anyone's guess.

I draw bugs and spiders, googley-eyes and long legs, the word *No. Definitely no.* I worry about the nurses seeing this and it adding to the list of reasons Seven and I belong here captive, but I keep sketching and rambling.

I don't like to think I can be broken, but that's what love is, right? A willingness to be a bead of blood, a sheaf of paper so thin you could tear it with a breath. But I can feel my heart reconstructing itself, resilient game of cat's cradle with each artery. I am winning. I'm trying to remember why I fell in love with Della, and if this is what love becomes. This exasperated feeling of resignation, a blind adoration like a dirty wind-shield I can't clear so I decide to taste instead. Tongue to glass, I can barely see out. I keep going. One frame in front of the other, blink by blink by swallow.

Della feels things profoundly, in a way she can't always articulate, but I can see it. This might explain her current incarceration. What might enter me as a soft sweet whisper could corrupt her week, could trap her under glass. Everything that bores, numbs and annoys me, she absorbs. Things terrify her at random. Sometimes she's fearless. To say she's unpredictable is the understatement of all time. She laughs out loud, so passionately sometimes that it knocks me to the ground. When you touch her, there is a palpable rawness. When she's asleep, I like to try to peer under her skin and see if someone accidentally put a city there, some sort of ancient civilization trapped where most of us have pores and hair follicles and derma papilla. Sometimes she is the girl who walks into the bar and everyone stares — men and women. They just look and look and get self-conscious and keep looking despite themselves. Other times she's the girl no one wants to look at, the crazy person on the bus who mutters to herself and stares at you in that way that she might ask you for the time or ask you if you've really loved your mother or could you touch her just to make sure she is really there. She's always been just this side of crazy, crazy enough to be an interesting artist, not disturbing enough for anyone to bother telling her to get help.

You know how people get, there could be a parade of indicators, a can-can line of girls screaming out *Your friend is obviously crazy!* but no one says a thing. *It's personal*, after all. You don't want to be the one to point it out and represent a bone-dry conventional world, one of doctors and chemicals and reality. It's so not punk rock. In fact, psychiatry is just another systemic oppression historically used to cure queers for being queer. Why embrace it? But I suppose Della had no choice. I'm ashamed to admit I'm somewhat relieved. I think I'm realizing, pushing a perfect hole for my thumb in the wrist of my shirt, everything is much more complicated than I'm willing to admit. Love. Craziness. All things in between.

I still like to watch her. After all these years, she can still amaze me as much as enrage me. Like when Rachel died, and she kept us all together. Somehow, she just knew what to do when no one else did. I know this afternoon is going to bring about an ending. This waiting room signifies more than I'm wanting to admit. I used to think that if I wasn't married to her or completely over her by the time I turned twenty-one, I was going to run away to the desert and join some sort of vaguely religious organization where all I had to do was make hammocks or spice racks all day, where things would be simple and clearly defined.

I draw a hammock, a crude illustration with Seven and I resting in it. I can't draw people. I don't pay enough attention to the details in their faces to properly represent them on paper. I know the other girl is in the cold hospital room with her, holding her hand. My jealousy is replaced by a calm resignation. *I'm no longer keeping score.*

2

THIS IS AN ORANGE

I'm consumed with imagining another woman curved around Della in an embrace. I am restless in my jealousy, but I can beat it. The score will be:

Jealousy: 0
Me: 1

I am trying to think about jealousy as an emotion the brain still has kicking around because our software is outdated. It once served some useful function, allowing us to survive and procreate, but now it causes drinks-in-the-face drama and tear-stained hangover breakfast heartbreak. All these things are so messy, no matter how many fastidious lists I make. You can't itemize emotions. They're messy like this room I'm sitting in, the ceiling with its streamers of spiderwebbing forming convoluted insect cities above our heads. Videotapes are strewn in front of the tiny square television sitting on top of a milk crate in the corner. Cases and tapes separate because last night it meant a lot that we find a tape of an old *Saturday Night Live* episode that was really funny. The one about chopping broccoli. We repeated it for hours, that ridiculous song. It's February, so we take fun where we can get it. It's in low supply, like serotonin and good hash; whereas PCP and depression, Montreal has in spades.

Jealousy is something I can overcome, if determined, and I am always very determined. It's impossible to sneeze and keep your eyes open at the same time, but I will master this as well. It's good to have a goal.

Tomato, Della's all-white cat, knows something is wrong. She's circling the perimeter of the room with dilated pupils, hair raised. I thought she was freaked out because earlier I was trying to do a handstand on two fingers. (It is possible.) But her anxiety is caused by something more than my erratic flailing about. Della came in when I was kicking my legs in the air and leaning against the wall upside down, trying to take away each finger slowly. She held me by the ankles as I giggled and squirmed, kissing her kneecaps with staccato smacks.

I'm eating a sloppy slice of tofu tortière from a plastic pink plate balanced precariously on my lap, cross-legged on Della's red armchair. The room is cold. Montreal is an angry ice cube. Between my cupped stocking feet is a green plastic two-litre bottle filled with peach juice crystals and tap water. I'm sticking two fingers into the cold, sugary liquid. They are slightly bruised from attempting to hold up all of me. It's Saturday at dusk. We stopped having sex because we forgot to eat. We forgot to stop looking at each other.

Tomato jumps over the discarded tapes and onto the coffee table, swerving her delicate body around the overflowing ashtrays, crusted-on plates, empty matchbooks. She emits a high-pitched meow, placing her eyes on mine in a lock.

Lassie, is Timmy in a well? I laugh, slightly unnerved.

I've been at Della's apartment since Wednesday, Valentine's Day. We'd made pink drinks in her blender and, though we both agreed the holiday was a celebration of corporate hetero-normativity, made the best of it like any couple still enraptured with each other.

She is lying on the futon couch, arms behind her head, watching the end scene from an afternoon movie, completely unconcerned with what Tomato is trying to communicate. Her short choppy blue hair a mass of curls, wearing a wife-beater and army pants, bare feet. At first glance, she'd look like a sixteen-year-old boy. With a closer look, from twenty-five to thirty, probably a girl. During a commercial she turns to me. "Are you ever going home?"

Her question startles me.

I mean, baby, I don't mind you being here.

Something about the way she says *baby*. Fucking caramel. A trap.

It's just that, well, you haven't been to work or gone home ...

Della hasn't gone to work, either. I don't point this out. Her job is vague and changes often. She's told me in quieter moments that sometimes she hates to be outside. It makes her star-eyed, heart-paused and falters her forward motion. The winter she was fifteen she didn't leave her house even once.

Della doesn't generally choose to be outside alone, or alone in general. She is most at ease in the middle of a cocktail party or a crowded dance floor at a bar. Her posture shifts, she's charming and warm, occasionally cocky. She has an anecdote for every silence. She lights up when she's insulated by a crowd. I don't think I have ever known her to spend an afternoon by herself. But I haven't known her all that long, I guess.

"Fine, I'll go." Getting up from the plush chair, I head towards the kitchen to rinse my plate. I sway my hips and flip my hair dramatically. I note that it is flip-length and this makes me happy in my goal to cultivate some femme-like status. With my scrawny torso, A-cups and slight hips, any physical femininity was going to come through my hair. I dyed it white blond last weekend. Another goal to get to. List it in a column. Check it off. Done.

"No, stay! I didn't mean to imply that you should leave. That's not what I meant."

Home is about three bus rides west to my parents' house, where I keep a simple bedroom half-packed-up in anxious anticipation of my Very Own Apartment. My mother cries when I mention the V.O.A. dream. She calls Della "that woman." *That woman* called. *That woman* is very rude on the phone, *that woman* doesn't even say hello.

Della's apartment is in the east end of the city, where Papineau and Ontario Street intersect, a part of the city I'd only ever visited to go to gay bars and, once, to get my tongue pierced while playing hooky during a grade nine field trip. The apartment is a minimal three-and-a-half with an eat-in kitchen, old moulded archways, the plaster on the ceilings in the shape of whipped cream swirls. Kitchen walls the Incredible Hulk could blend into seamlessly. Silver doorways and kitchen cupboards. Hot pink bathroom that screams at you while you pee. One living-room wall is orange, another red and two are bright blue. It's like living in the middle of an exploding comet. Mannequin parts are everywhere, jointed arms and legs strewn about. Her bathroom is covered in doll parts and toys hot glued to every surface. Her bedroom is all white with a simple black wool blanket on a futon bed. One full-length mirror. A shelf from IKEA holding some books. A drawing table. There is one poster, on the wall above her bed, featuring big-busted amazons from a Russ Myers movie, advertising a popular weekly dyke night at a bar in the village.

If I go home, I'm not certain when I will see Della again. She lives in the extreme present. When I am in front of her, I am certain that I am beautiful; I am wanted. When I am tapping my fingers on the cash register at work or standing at school waiting to fill up my travel mug with hot black coffee, thinking of our last kiss, she could be anywhere, kissing anyone, my fingers far from her thoughts. I don't have bad self-esteem, I'm realistic.

This is what we call a Revolutionary Relationship: depending on our own conventions, not falling into traps set by expectations, codependency and unreasonable romanticism.

No definitions.

The trouble with deciding not to define anything is that it usually means you have to talk a lot more about what you're not defining than you would if you employed the time-honoured grade nine approach to Going Steady.

I will be fine with our ultra-postmodern relationship. It isn't anything but what it needs to be right now. I always leave my mark, rubbing against the walls like Tomato, leaving a trail. Lip-gloss prints on her wine glasses. From the bed to the bathroom: my dropped crumbs, my lighter, a scribbled phone number on an envelope. A towel. My gloves. I give extra-long goodbye hugs. She never answers her phone. I forget to check my voicemail messages. We may as well live in different countries.

When my textbooks are open in my lap, trudging through Foucault or Butler, reading the same sentence over and over again, wondering if I'm secretly mentally retarded and no one ever bothered to tell me, I pick up a pen and go on and on in the margins about love being a terribly boring preoccupation, a convention, a construct. That's when I know things are not going well. I press my palms to my bulging eyes. I forget to flinch when I should, instead I embrace each bright light moment that is Della. Then I feel as though I've been snapped up like a bug in her net.

On our first real date she served me hash brownies from a crumpled napkin in her coat pocket when she picked me up outside St-Laurent Metro. I kissed her face and giggled. We went to a warehouse party on Ontario Street where Della knew everyone. I drank martinis from these oversized pink plastic martini glasses that a gorgeous drag queen named Mabel kept bringing to me. "You're just a tiny little angel!"

she'd say, and hand me a new one. "I can't even believe you're allowed to be here. I have shoes older than you!" I stood up front dancing while a band called The Snitches played. They were mesmerizing. The drummer was a woman with a shaved head and lip piercing and the singer had more energy than anyone I'd ever seen. I fell in love. I was under some sort of spell and I didn't want it to end.

Walking to the party she told me she was only going to live for two more years, tops. Not one woman from her mother's family has lived past the age of thirty. It's a Johnson curse. Della turns thirty next year. We are just under ten years apart. She's hoping that her father's tough Tremblay genes will win. Her mother died when Della was twelve years old. Cancer. I didn't know what to say when she told me that. I think I said sorry. Not a good enough thing to say, but I couldn't think of anything more appropriate. I remember thinking how weird it was — how much she divulged to me so quickly. One of her many quirks, I suppose.

I find it hard enough to say even the basic things I'm thinking. For some reason they stick to the roof of my mouth, dissolve before they turn from emotion to language.

I stayed that night at her place, drunk, giggling and falling into the bright walls. Della was the kind of untouchable cool you never think you'll get close to, and then you're stretched over her naked body, but you're still not close yet. The next morning I walked to the subway and the cool fall air was a baptism.

The first time I met Della, she was wearing a white wife-beater tank top. She'd scrawled *boy beater* across the chest in red marker. The shirt showed off her muscled arms painted in two bright sleeves of tattoos. She was wearing baggy green army pants and had scraggly blue and black hair that was moulded and pointed in peaks like she was straight out of a comic book. At first glance I wasn't sure if she was a boy or a girl and it didn't matter. I was slack-jawed and near tour-retic and trying unsuccessfully to hide it.

She was helping my art teacher in CEGEP hang our first-semester student vernissage, painting benches for visitors to sit on in blue and silver. We had a moment at the oversized sink, washing our hands. I couldn't look at her, I felt her watching my hands, watching the colours bleed into the running warm water. I couldn't figure out if my hands were still a part of my body, I stared so hard. I felt her beside me like a wall of white light, an eclipsing moon. I felt the same way I did when I hid under the blankets during *The Exorcist*. I just couldn't trust my eyes with her. She was too much to absorb. She broke the moment with a laugh. *I think your hands are clean now, baby*. The way she said *baby*, so pre-sumptuous, like she was holding all the answers in her hands instead of several long paint brushes.

We've been dating, or whatever, for almost two months now. A relationship starting in January in this cold city shouldn't feel so optimistic, it should feel practical and insulating. But it doesn't. The winter can't touch this.

Della's apartment exists inside a rip in the space-time continuum. I feel as though if I can stay still in the valley of thrift-store furniture hugged by the bright walls on Cartier Avenue, I can rest. Whenever I feel like it I can jump back into the rotating skipping rope: my life. Living out of my knapsack is a strange comfort. The folds of canvas fabric are my own four walls. Kept and containing.

It feels like we are waiting for something. Like we can sense the impending explosion.

I crawl back into the armchair. We stare at each other, from the cat, to the TV, to the couch. I don't want to leave because I'm comfortable. I am also replaceable. The fingerprints on the door handles, the cutlery, the wine glasses, Della's belt buckle, they aren't all mine.

Before we started this hibernation holiday, we'd gone out to launder the sheets on Thursday, after an overnight date. Hungover and hopelessly honeymooning, we fucked against the washing machines while an old man slept in the corner of the laundromat.

When we arrived back at her apartment, giddy and high, Della patted down her jeans pockets, the inside of her coat, closed her eyes tightly and exhaled a frustrated sigh. She'd left her keys inside. We were locked out.

"Why don't you keep a copy under the mat?"

Della rolled her eyes.

"No problem, we'll break in the back room." Della is one of those people who could state something outrageous, like *I can eat a light bulb*, and say it with such conviction, you'd immediately believe her. Later you might find a burning question mark abandoned in your stomach.

In the alleyway behind Cartier Avenue, a tiny corridor peppered with puddles and litter, she tried to wedge her body into the hole in her apartment wall.

"Why do you have a hole in your apartment wall?"

The circular hole from the alley into the apartment was the size of a basketball. It was filled with pink fibreglass insulation, brown fabric quilted in triangles, the skeleton of an old coat. Della was skinny with no hips to speak of, but I really didn't think she could get through without the help of a genie in a magic lamp.

"The landlord told me the old tenants stole the dryer, and this is where the air filtered out. He never filled it in or bothered to get a new one. That's why I only pay $300 for the place." Her voice was muffled inside the hole. I ran my hand up her legs. "Stop it!" she giggled.

I could hear that we'd left a CD on in the living room. It was skipping. Portishead's *Dummy*.

Della removed her head and arms from the hole and exhaled in defeat, pieces of dust and dirt clung to her sweaty forehead. She tells me, with some reluctance in her voice, that we're going to have to go to xxxx's house. "She has an extra key." Della looked away deliberately, fiddling with her clothes, pretending she didn't normally avoid saying xxxx's name around me. "Baby, don't give me that look."

"What look?" I firmed my face into complete non-reaction. xxxx's name is too evil to write or say out loud. It's the kind of name that blinds you. xxxx is the Other Lover and she lives ten or twelve blocks towards the almost frozen Rive Sud.

She had a key? I didn't have a key. I had Della's hand pulsing near all of my precious internal organs thirteen minutes before we discovered this problem, but no key to her home.

I held the plastic laundry hamper in my hands, Della carried the red hockey bag on her back. We walked in silence away from the abandoned break-in mission and towards where xxxx lived.

xxxx was Della's real girlfriend, wife even, for five years, when Della used to do things like have girlfriends, before she learned it was important not to imply ownership with labels and restrictions. Della insists she is not even one bit in love with xxxx anymore. Occasionally they still sleep together, but it's *no big deal, just habit.* When I tell her I feel like the *other woman*, she laughs. *That's just learned sexist bullshit. We are all in charge of our own bodies and what we decide to do with them. We are all our own.*

I believed it when she said it, like she'd opened up a new valve that had been stuck. I felt unconfined and open-minded and totally confused. Intellectually, non-monogamy made complete sense; emotionally, it felt like sandpaper across my eyelids.

Arriving at xxxx's apartment, it was almost cold enough for me to feel relieved. We climbed cautiously to the third floor on a twisted iron staircase, caked in ice, that curled around in front of a three-storey red brick apartment building. xxxx opened the door after three long rings of the tinny doorbell as Della and I stood in complete silence, indicating our hollow need. She was wearing a red towel. She blushed at Della with a smirk that faded when she saw my small frame hovering beside her. Or maybe I imagined that. Maybe she doesn't have hang-ups.

In a towel, she was a stunning woman. Long black curls, muscled arms, feminine lips, small curves. Real. She is a real woman and I am a child.

I am invisible. I willed this to happen. If I believed in God, which I do sometimes, I would say *please God, make me invisible.* My relationship with God is like my relationship to vegetarianism. I eat bacon at 11:15; at 11:18, I stop. Then I am a vegetarian again. I don't believe in God. But when I need something, there He is. Please, just this once. I feel like I might eventually grow out of this kind of perfunctory infantile spiritual relationship to the world, but so far, He was still some Santa Claus Polaroid at my imaginary disposal during a crisis.

I studied my feet carefully. They looked like baby feet. Why did I wear pink platform sneakers? Under my coat I wore a snug, white Sonic Youth baby tee, baggy skater pants stolen from my last boyfriend. I patted my head to see if I left the plastic baby barrettes at home. No such luck. They were mortifyingly the ones with little ducks and stars on them. I wanted to bolt. But I'd left my wallet in Della's apartment and had no money, no keys to my own house.

Della explained to xxxx, in French, that we'd left our keys in the apartment, we were freezing our asses off, *est-ce qu'on peût fumer a l'interieur?*

xxxx invited us in with all the decorum of a proper English hostess who'd been expecting diplomats for tea. She walked with a side-to-side sway in her hips, barefoot and in a towel. If I tried this, the effect would be ridiculous.

There was no etiquette for this situation. I read *The Ethical Lesbian's Guide to Polyamory* but it was way too West-Coast-New-Age to make any sense to me. How do you find time to have sex with all that discussion? Della and I sat on the plush couch while xxxx disappeared into her room and re-emerged moments later in a black blouse and jeans.

xxxx and I looked at each other with the strained effort of those who try desperately to match their political belief in polyamory with their emotional need to be warm at night. Sleeping soundly with the knowledge that you are someone's every need and want fulfilled is a hard thing to give up, even if it is ultimately a lie, a game of Scrabble without enough vowels and the salt-filled timer discarded and unused.

We small-talked the paintings on her wall (her own — a pastiche of pastel goddesses — yuck), the AIDS art show she was organizing called *Day Without Art* and the impending storm. My hands thawed. xxxx emptied a desk drawer onto the living room floor, trying to find the extra key.

When xxxx bent over to paw through the drawer's contents I noticed her ass. It was faultless, two perfect teacups. My hatred and jealousy was ... turning me on? I pinched the inside of my right arm to avoid the awkward eroticism. I'd never been with another girly-girl before, this was an odd moment, to feel so gay. I stared at the protest signs leaning in a clump in the corner of her room. They had hand prints on them with the text *The government has blood on their hands.* I looked around the giant double living room and office, messy, filled with books and objects I recognized. Her furniture wasn't from IKEA. It was oak, teak, cherrywood, solid and shining. Antique and sturdy. The kind of furniture my mother talks about buying, but never does. Her couch was L shaped, the kind of fluffy you sink into for days — but can just jump out of. xxxx had cash. I expected her place was going to be like a girl version of Della, less comic book, more organized, more reds than earth tones.

"Well, I was just fixing some food, if you guys are hungry."

Della grunted something that sounded like yes. xxxx left us to an awkward silence. I picked up her copy of *Slingshot*, an anarchist newspaper. Della turned on the TV. It felt like we were polite strangers in a waiting room.

xxxx came out with a tray of shrimp, like a shrimp roll or whatever they are called, as though she had expected us. What's next, finger sandwiches? Tiny spring rolls? She offered me one first. When was the last time I made anything that wasn't encased in plastic from a microwave?

"No thanks ... allergic." I lied. Something about taking anything from her didn't sit well.

"Oh. Had a strange craving this morning and took these out of the freezer." She offered one to Della, who bit into it with a snap.

"The shrimp's heart is in its head you know," Della said, holding the tail like a cigarette filter. She bit sharply. They shared a look only people who've known each other for years can. But I sat, with my nipples hard through my thin shirt, aware that at eighteen, I was the reason women like Della decided to open their relationships.

I thought about how I was going to be eighteen for another week. Turning nineteen on February 20 would be a quiet victory. Della thought I was twenty. "You look like jail bait," she'd said, taking my hand at the bar. Yeah, I get that a lot. I still use the fake ID I've had since I was sixteen, for consistency, which would now make me twenty.

I keep my impending adulthood to myself, staying quiet when she says things like, *You're like a cross between Ginger and Mary-Ann from* Gilligan's Island and I don't know what she's talking about.

I got up to rinse my cup and snoop around the kitchen. xxxx had a lot of garlic hanging on the walls, an empire of tea boxes displayed in a cupboard with glass doors, dried herbs in mason jars labelled *nettle tea, pennyroyal tea* (that's where Nirvana got that song title, I noted), *lavender, green tea, detox herbs*. Her fridge door displayed a collage of postcards that said things like, *Your body is a battleground. Stonewall was a riot, not a brand name. Against Abortion? Have a Vasectomy. We're Here, We're Queer, We're Not Going Shopping*, and QUEER NATION. When I turned the water off, I heard her saying, "Now I know why you didn't want me to meet her, Della. What is she, some fucking baby dyke kid from NDG or some shit?"

"She's twenty ... from Dorval, I think."

"Is she, like, even fucking gay, like for real, or is she like, curious?"

xxxx began to swear in French and make disapproving clicks with her tongue. "What could you possibly see in ..." She flows between French and English seamlessly, like it's all one language. xxxx has a French mother and an English father, only her mother was more assimilated into English culture, because her father was old money from Westmount. Apparently xxxx has been exiled since she came out. I walked back through the living room, interrupting to ask where the bathroom was. She motioned me down the hall towards the front door and to the left. I walked slowly, peering into her open bedroom door. My heart pounded while I stood staring at her unmade bed, the clothes strewn across the floor. Her room like splayed legs relaxed with the assumption of no onlookers. I blush, seeing she's left a plate with half-eaten apple slices beside the bed. A cup of water turned on its side, drooling onto her dresser top, leaves a stain like a ninth-grade hickey, a first-degree burn. There is a leather sling hooked up in the corner and a giant wooden cross with wrist and ankle restraints attached. *Wow*, I thought, giggling, before pausing to wonder if this is what Della is into. What if I was too boring for her?

In the bathroom I noted several tubes of age-defying moisturizers, eyelash curlers, a row of vitamins, homeopathic pills and kava kava. I pocketed a tube of bright red lipstick, ran a smear of moisturizer under my eyes.

I walked slowly back into the living room, pretending to be absorbed in a bookcase. A lot of books about women and witches. I sucked in my tummy, stuck out my tits and ran my finger seductively over *Sisterhood Is Powerful*.

xxxx looked into my eyes with rehearsed ambivalence. It was hard to hold her gaze without accepting defeat with a shy giggle. It hit me then, that I may have the perky tits and the soft skin, but she had the power. She looked like she didn't need Della.

xxxx and I had never officially met, but you could not be queer in this town and be unaware of her. Small-c queer celebrity, reputation as a heartbreaker and a pretty successful sculptress and painter. When you see someone shouting on the news at demonstrations, the camera always focuses on her. She gives good sound bites. The journalists pick up on her last name, because of her father, I suppose, the name they recognize from City Hall bylines. I imagine it must infuriate them further.

I got all this dish from Melanie, my women's studies classmate and unofficial lesbian community research adviser. Word on the street is that Della always cheated, even with xxxx's best friends. xxxx walked into the bar on dyke night, sashayed up to the former best friend who'd slept with Della the night before and punched her in the face. This was before their breakup and consequent ex-sex / undefined relationship. When monogamy was still cool enough.

I knew a lot about her, she knew only my exterior; the smell of my hair (coconut), vaguely size 8, short, A-cups, pale, quiet. A polite smile.

Melanie and I would often sit at that same bar, years after the rumoured punch-out, and watch xxxx in our periphery as she served drinks and looked stunning. I usually made Melanie order the drinks so I'd never have to speak to her. Melanie seemed to know everything about everyone who had ever even thought about kissing another girl on the island of Montreal. I told her she should open up her own supersleuth ace-girl dyke detective agency. She got most of her info because she was sleeping with her women's studies teacher.

I'd be lying if I didn't admit how fascinated I was with xxxx. She made my heart race and my mouth somewhat slack, pupils wider than necessary to take in light. Not hate, not a crush — jealous, definitely, but also keenly interested. I am forging this new life of queers and artists and adulthood, and here is this example of someone I could become. She created these paradoxical feelings, like I might want to study her, or kick her in the shins. Unlike Della, who simply made me feel as though I was perpetually on the verge of ignition. One look, one exhale on my neck, and I was flattened.

I turned back to Della and xxxx, who were done eating. Della smoked. She didn't seem nervous, but I wondered if she was, if she felt awkward. The awkwardness seemed to be me. I noticed a scar on her neck I hadn't noted before. I watched her inhale. Exhale. Like all verses and no chorus. xxxx had flawless skin. I made a note to buy all those moisturizers in the future. So much poise to spare. I needed some. I could feel spontaneous zits forming in the middle of my face. xxxx looked like she could be one of those girls in a shampoo commercial. Lint and cat hair would just fall off of her. She never had ripped hemlines or cigarette burns on her sleeves. Everything I had was imperfect in some way. I come by it honestly — my parents were more creative and messy than efficient, taught me to wipe my hands on my jeans, pin things up when the buttons drop off, buy second-hand clothes.

I felt shy when xxxx looked at me. Shy doesn't cut it, really, more like eraseable chalk dust after being wiped down by an underpaid math teacher. I was an idea. Now I am almost clean and blank, my fingers feel powdery.

Della stood casually, announcing that we should probably get going, as if we had dinner plans or something, instead of just an assumption that there would be more sex, maybe some pills, a movie, start that over again. While they hugged goodbye, I stuffed a lacy, red g-string between her couch cushions. Obviously mine, because Della only wore boy's briefs. xxxx probably never wore underwear. Too patriarchal.

As soon as we were outside, warm and nicotine-satiated, key in hand, Della explained that xxxx had the key to her apartment for security reasons. She was afraid to be alone at night. I rolled my eyes. xxxx looked like she was more dangerous than a carving knife. Serrated edges on all of her perfectly articulated words. She looked like she could snap Della in half with a smirk.

"What if I was sleeping over?"

"Well, she wouldn't actually use the key, Evie. She just likes to know that she could — this neighbourhood isn't that safe. She lives alone. You know how it is. And besides, we're like family."

I nodded because I wanted to seem as though I did know how it is. I was barely ten years old when they met. I am not old enough to have had a lover for eight years or to know what it's like to live alone and be lonely.

I don't know what to say. I let the quiet settle between us. I do not exclaim much. I'm not usually one to take what is swirling around in my gut to mean anything specific. I am not a good translator. I think this is why my friends growing up were mostly boys. They expected less conversation about anything not currently in front of them.

Do you remember that game at summer camp? *This is an orange. A what? An orange.* You pass an orange around in a circle and you have to keep repeating that. I'm not sure what this is supposed to accomplish — heathly group dynamics or something. This is how I feel now. Like I should look at her and say, *This is a challenge. A what? A Challenge. These are my confessions. Your what? Confessions.*

But I don't.

Jealousy is too irrational a feeling to make sense of. Like trying to explain why you like the colour blue. You just do. I just want xxxx to die. Simple. Or, more truthfully, less exaggeratedly, I want her to want. To wonder. To feel lack.

I hope that if anything, this jealousy will toughen my heart until it feels like a dollar-store bottle rocket. Common, sturdy, but still potentially explosive. Like anybody else. Even though everyone gets jealous, even if you're adept at fronting like you don't, jealousy makes people ordinary and weak. At the same time, when you're feeling it in the most extreme way you worry you might become a murderer, someone controlled by passion and ego. In France they have lesser sentences for those who kill out of passion. Passion is a reasonable excuse to lose track of your moral core. Crazy. xxxx made me crazy. xxxx made me feel like my heart was the first heart ever to feel this way. Solitary struggling to hold its ground at the top of the organ hierarchy.

When we got home and unlocked the door, Della lay back on the couch, turned on the TV with her toe. She pulled back the tin lever from a can of pudding. Gobs of butterscotch filled in the tense spaces. We settled in. Hours passed. Baths. Sex. Sleep. I baked vegan cookies in the shape of superheroes. I just poured in ingredients without measuring anything, handful of sugar, vegetable oil, mashed up frozen banana I found next to the bottle of vodka and the ice cubes. Smoked pot. Ate the cookies. Watched TV.

Now I sit in the chair with another piece of pseudo-tortière sizzling from three minutes in the microwave. Ketchup puddles on the side. We're back to where we started. Eating, the cat freaking out, the weird feelings.

I bring the green bottle to my lips and suck. I cough. Della licks the spoon from another cup of pudding and throws it on the floor when she's done. From twenty-eight to four in half a second. Tomato runs over to it, swatting it with her paws.

"No baby, I want you to stay. Stay!" She gets up and attacks me with a giggling hug. We fall to the sticky floor and kiss.

Now that she wants me to stay, I decide to go — I'm hopelessly predictable. I don't mind being average and horrible at love. I pull away from our entanglement and get up to walk quickly into her room. "Why? You don't have to go, seriously, *bébé*! It was just a question!"

I peel off my two-day-old Hello Kitty underwear, root through self-help books, art books and empty cigarette packs for a clean pair of hers. She stands in the doorway watching and pouting, lower lip protruding, eyes playful and apologetic. One hand on hip, the other on her head, impossibly charming.

I feel unable to hold back from asking how she met xxxx, to fake cool disinterest any longer.

"It's kind of tacky, really. So cliché."

"What, at a potluck? A solstice gathering?"

She stood in the doorway watching me get dressed, her head bent slightly to one side, looking me up and down, arms crossed in a maybe.

"I worked construction in my early twenties. I helped build a deck at her parents' house in Westmount."

"Are you joking? That's such a porno movie!"

"I know! She was engaged to some asshole guy. She was on the student government at McGill."

"And look at her now ... you corrupted her!"

Della laughed. "Well, the feminists got their hands on her, too." She said. "Let me show you something." She fumbles through her desk drawer and pulls out a photo. Della is barely recognizable wearing overalls with a women's symbol painted on the front flap and a black T-shirt, sporting a short crew cut in what appears to be her natural hair colour. She only has one tattoo on her arm where there are now sleeves of colour. Della quickly covers it up with her thumb. Beside her is ...

"Oh my God, that's not xxxx?!" The person with her arms around Della has short choppy hair, a veritable hockey-hair mullet. She's wearing a ripped, white tank top, ugly, red cotton pants and sandals. They're tanned and standing in front of a tent.

"That was us in Michigan in ..." She turns over the photo and scrawled in pen is *Summer 1989*. "We were twenty-two."

"That's some bad fashion!"

"It was the eighties ..."

I've burned all my Hammer pants and glittery vests, so there's no proof of my Naughty By Nature phase.

She hands me another one, a crowd scene with many shaved-headed queers holding picket signs.

"This is us at the protests against the Sex Garage attacks in ... '90 ... the same summer of the ..."

"Oka crisis." I finish for her, remembering the helicopters over our house, the army on the bridge, my mother yelling at the television.

"What was Sex Garage?"

"A warehouse party the cops busted up ... they beat the shit out of all these fags and dykes. It was unbelievable. That's where I got this from." She pointed to a scar on her lower leg. "From a baton." The scar looked deep and rubbery.

"Holy shit."

"Yeah, they just walked in, I was working the door and suddenly all these cops just came in and walked around and stared at everyone. Then they left. I was like, 'Fuck, that's not going to be the end of that,' so I got ready to leave, and suddenly they showed up and they ripped their nametags off, and just started beating the shit out of everyone. My friend Ashton was leaving in a cab and they surrounded the cab and dragged him out of the back seat and kicked him so hard he had to go to the hospital. He almost died."

"What the fuck? Just 'cause they were having a party? How many fucking raves have I been to in the suburbs the cops don't ever touch?"

"Yeah, well, the community organized right away. It got worse before it got better. We were just peacefully protesting outside the police station and they dragged my friend into the station by her hair. They took my other friend out the back of the station in an ambulance when it was clear they'd really fucked him up."

"Huh."

I vaguely remember news footage on television from those protests. I was fifteen, sitting between my parents on the couch after dinner trying to catch a glimpse of all those gay people in the same place.

Della kneels on the side of the bed now, her scraggly blue-black hair sticking straight up. I stopped getting dressed because I was too absorbed in the story. Tracing her fingers along my legs, she makes car noises. I lie back and she sits at the end of the bed, smiling. There is a silent wave of potential sex happening, but first we want to smoke. I stick a cigarette in my mouth, she reaches into her pocket and pulls out her Zippo lighter engraved with the word "dream" on it and reaches out to light it.

The sound that a bomb makes brings to mind no exact words. With the swish of her lighter, I inhale, and take in the explosion four apartments south. It's like an elevator plunging, and your ears popping and someone walking into you with a lit cigarette, all simultaneously. Then it's over. Leaving us with a shallow stream of broken glass on the other side of the bed, our hands clasped together, the cigarette burning a slow hole in her duvet, an opera of car alarms going off in unison all over the neighbourhood.

3

BLUE-BLACK SLUGS

The building settles and shakes like a person coming down from a seizure. All the windows are shattered up and down the block. A woman is screaming, swearing. Sirens approach what seems almost instantly. More urgently than usual.

Upheaval is a steady exhale in this neighbourhood — red lights and red eyes. But this is different. Car alarms continue to blare like experimental techno. Dogs bark in chorus. Tomato sprints up and down the hall and then ducks under the bed.

We look at each other. Our faces haven't changed.

"*Hostie collis*! ..." Della swears. "Are you okay?"

Our hearts are accordions. I slip into jeans and a wool sweater, the first things I find with my hands, itchy against bare skin. The power is out. It's still light out but the darkness of her apartment makes it hard to see. I follow her wordlessly as she scuffles five steps ahead of me, trying unsuccessfully to get her right foot into an orange Converse sneaker, through the front door. We head south towards Ontario Street in a stumbling jog.

The southwest corner is in flames. What were a tattoo shop and a bar seem to be unravelling like a red bundle of yarn pouring smoke upwards. Thick grey-black cream. Strangers speculate, talking in fast French that I don't catch all of. Della gathers everyone around the cops, who are tight-lipped, crime scenes normalized in their skin. The fire trucks block everything, we can't tell if anyone's been hurt.

It's cold. Colder than it has been. I think I have attention deficit disorder because I want to leave; my interest has piqued and descended. I want to be holding Della in bed. People stand, staring, wanting to stay till the credits roll.

The apartment looks different from the outside. The front window is shattered. Another fucking hole.

I fall asleep to the ripping and folding sound of Della taping up the window with industrial duct tape. In the morning I wake up feeling anxious. I see she's drawn skulls of warning for potential intruders. The apartment is now just a tent in a rainstorm instead of a force that keeps the bad things out and the comfortable home in. Della is making calls to the landlord, whose phone appears to have been disconnected. I feel as though my left and right legs were switched in my sleep. We both take a Valium with our cream of wheat. One of Della's many former jobs included cleaning up houses where old people died. Her medicine cabinet reads like a phone book of unfamiliar names fading on plastic vials.

Della's brother, who works as a contractor, arrives to fix the window. We watch the midday news while smoothing down slabs of hardened brown sugar into a milky bowl with plastic spoons. *A biker bomb*, says news anchor Dennis Trudeau. We look for ourselves in the news footage. We don't see us.

I refill the pop bottle with red flavouring, hold it under the tap until it overflows, staining my hands pink. It reminds me of the colour of those cherry-flavoured pills dentists give you when you're a kid to show you where you have plaque.

It's the Valium that prohibits me from leaving today. It's creating this illusion that inside is safe and the landscape outside is precarious at best. Della and I are merging physically. From her elbow to my thigh. Her lips to my soft arches. Della calls in sick to work again. Do I care that I haven't been alone in six days? Is love supposed to feel like needing another lung?

It doesn't feel completely right, her and me. But everything else feels far away.

I fall asleep and wake up with the pills worn off. My heart is pounding. I'm having a heart attack. My teeth feel like charcoal.

"Baby, no one has a heart attack when they're twenty. Take another Ivan."

We call the Valium *Ivan*, because that is who it was pre-scribed for. Ivan McAllister. Lived alone in Outremont. Died of a heart attack. I settle into the couch, fade out at the edges. The morning greets me with a kick. A pain in my side. I feel all the pebbles I've swallowed.

My mother calls the number she found scrawled on a paper in my jeans pocket. Della looks confused when she hears the high-pitched maternal voice on the end of the line. She drops the receiver in my lap like a question mark.

"Where are you? I called Jenny and she has no idea where you are."

Jenny is my best friend from high school. Despite being the biggest bad-ass kid in our neighbourhood, she's managed to maintain a perpetual angelic façade around my mother, who thinks of her as a second daughter, even when she's coming down off of a mescaline bender on our couch. My mother brings her soup for her terrible flu and lets her watch all the crime shows even though they make her nervous.

Jenny, tall and empirically beautiful and therefore suspect, was regarded by my principal, the minister at church and everyone but my mother, as a *handful*. I really like how gentle and open-minded my mother is with Jenny. I think that she relates to her in a way, because she ran away from her religious family at fifteen and didn't look back. She understands being an outsider.

I was great accomplice material for Jenny. Quiet.

In grade ten Jenny and I came home so drunk that she spent the night crying and throwing up in the basement bathroom. My mother held her hair and made maternal circles on her back comforting her, listening to her go on about Andrew who was a jerkface liar scumbag. My mother was so kind and patient with her.

The next day she said, "Eve, you better not be doing drugs or drinking. I'll ground you till you're forty-five." I had the sense there would be no hair-holding privileges for me should I ever admit my non-sobriety to her.

I could hear my mother tapping a pen impatiently against the list she was writing. "So, where are you?"

"I'm downtown. At my friend Della's."

"Who is this Della again?"

"A friend from art class."

"Oh, yes, her. Well, you know, if you never call and you never come home, your father and I worry."

Something like a clanging tambourine or a small chewing animal starts dancing in my stomach.

"Well, I'm okay." You're going to have to let go some time, I'm eighteen.

"Good." You're still a kid.

"How are you? How's Dad?" I decide not to tell her about my proximity to the bomb that went off, even though it's all I can talk about to anyone else I speak to.

"We're fine."

"Oh yeah."

"He needs your help with inventory you know, he's been giving all your shifts to Alex."

My dad owns a music store. I've been working there since I was twelve.

"Alex needs the money and everything, so he doesn't mind. But you've got to shape up. He can't make exceptions for you just cause you're the boss's kid."

"Sorry."

"Well, you know, it's quiet around here without you and Jenny running around."

My mother was perhaps lonely.

"Well, I'll come home tonight, okay?"

"Oh, it doesn't matter. Whenever. You know, I just wanted to know you were okay."

"Yup." I curl the phone cord around my finger impatiently.

When I hang the phone up, Della looks amused.

"She worries too much," I say. "I can't wait till I can afford my own place."

I walk around the apartment gathering up all my things and stuffing them arbitrarily into my heavy canvas knapsack. School books, dirty red socks, my stinky one-stars, a book Della lent me about lesbian culture called *Dyke Life*. It's overflowing so I put some things in a white plastic grocery bag. Della walks me to the subway. Della's eyes dart, her face is flushed.

"Are you okay?" I ask her after we hug goodbye.

"Yeah. I'm fine." She's not, but I'm not sure what I should do about it. I turn to walk into the station, the handles of the plastic bags forming angry, red half-circles on my palms.

I push the sticky play button on my red cassette Walkman. "She's Crushing My Mind" by Team Dresch floods my brain and, as if hypnotized by the ragged harmonies, I'm clutching my cardboard transfer to show the driver, finding another seat and somewhat suddenly finding myself at home. Dreamy and swaying. I kick my wet boots into the pile by the door of our duplex and walk wordlessly up the carpeted stairs straight into my room. The house smells like oregano and brewed coffee and vanilla candles.

I don't know what to do, sitting on my bed, curled up, suddenly exhausted. I try to read for school but can't concentrate. I make half a mixed tape for Della, carefully planning each song with coded messages of my devotion.

My mother eventually ends her silence with a warm smile, standing in the doorway of my room, inviting me down to eat. She seems to have missed me. She feeds me well with potatoes and green vegetables. Thick food that gathers my insides up and makes everything work together towards life. She doesn't even try to make me eat the ham or make any remarks about my hair. She's wearing a new sweater. I tell her it's pretty. Evens the score. We hug.

I do the dishes while my dad sits at the table taking apart an old synthesizer, the sound of an episode of *Roseanne* emanating from the living room.

It seems no one in the west end is worried about bombs, only the impending fear that if Quebec separates we'll be forced to move to Cornwall or Kingston.

After dinner, in the peach-and-yellow wallpapered bathroom, I put my hands against the yellow sink. I vow my own apartment would look like it wasn't still the seventies. No fake wood panelling, no wallpaper. I look into the mirror, my pupils outlined with a red pencil crayon, blue-black slugs under my eyes. I can feel how Della held me this morning while waking; her tongue teasing my thighs. I blush at my own memory. No one had ever made me feel that much all at once. I fill the tub with lavender bath salts and scorching hot water. Light candles. Finally feel myself returning to me.

I settle under the covers, feeling a sudden exhaustion — perhaps a result of the Valium bender. I dial seven numbers, pink chipped nail polish pressing each button down with firm resolve. I want not to be needy, but I want to call Della to say goodnight, my right hand sliding underneath my PJ pants.

xxxx answers. "Hey, Eve." There is a pause so long she has to know it's purposeful. Making me wait for her to pass the phone to Della. Blood frozen in place. "She'll call you back," she says, coyly, quick. Was she breathless? Did she show up right after I left, was my spot on the couch even cold?

My vision thrown off, all I see are targets. I fall deeper into my quilted bed. Fade out again. I sit up straight, every limb a plywood plank. I pull the tape out of my ghetto blaster and throw it across the room. I set to work imagining, tracing xxxx's thigh. My mental tongue is getting started when I am stunned awake: I've developed a crush on this girl who loves Della.

I hate it when rational thought interrupts fantasy.

It's unavoidable, this erotic space of want. I want something from her, it may as well be her. When I do get her, I'm going to slyly grind her leg into mine on the dance floor, a sword fight of silent coyness. When I kiss her neck it will be jealousy transformed. It is just a feeling but now it is tangible.

Jenny used to do this: sleep with all of my boyfriends, when I was fourteen and holding tight to some myth about saving myself for the right person. As if virginity was a shiny gold coin with endless value. Jenny thought that was bullshit and would give the boys what they wanted, what she wanted. I remember her turning to me after she let me go on about *should I or shouldn't I* let a boy get in my pants. She said, "Eve, for fuck's sake. Madonna said losing her virginity was a good career move. I see it that way, too."

At the end of a night of partying, ripping her stockings open with a long nail, she'd say, "I just do it to get close to you," and close her door, passing out behind it. My boyfriends were apologetic but helpless. I would immediately lose interest in them. She was always too strong a pull.

I would take my keys and scratch a pattern into Jenny's heavy metallic apartment door, jagged lightning highs and lows like my pulse, signalling alive alive alive alive alive, the door looked hated. I was always the one sober enough to walk her home, make sure she was okay. The patterns looked hateful, but they weren't. Her mother always remarked, *Delinquents in this neighbourhood!*

Jenny calls, I reach my hand out from under the covers. "Hey freak, what are you doing for your nineteenth birthday?"

"I dunno. It's not like it's a big-deal birthday." I tell her about xxxx.

"You know what your problem is? You concentrate too much on her. Go out and get laid, make her jealous. I'm going to take you out and we'll get drunk and find you some ass ... there's got to be hotter girls out there you haven't met. Deal?"

"Deal. Except I hate dyke bars. The music sucks."

"We'll go out on St-Laurent then. I know! We'll go see the Breeders. I can get John to let us in the side door."

Jenny has a special relationship with almost every bouncer in town.

Somehow I predict we'll just get drunk at the Bifteque and by last call we'll be making out with the same boys in the same bands we've been kissing since grade ten, hands smelling like free popcorn and breath raging with Boreal and tequila shooters. If there is a dyke in the bar, she'll try to pick up Jenny. Jenny has the kind of beauty that stops cars. If Jenny didn't sneer at Della, I'd never let her near her. I think Jenny's trying to make up for the ninth-grade plays for my boyfriends by feigning disinterest in Della. Or perhaps it's the old adage about hating the people who remind us of ourselves — Della was really the butchy-dyke equivalent of Jenny, the stopping-cars tomboy, making every girl with a slight proclivity towards queerness fawn. Look at her muscled forearms, drool. Look at her dispassionate lack of engagement, kiss me!

Della knows more than she lets on. I call her back and let it ring and ring and ring some more. Every ring enrages me. Pretending that she doesn't know what's going on is not satisfying to me. The imagined bite on xxxx's thigh, this will bring it home. She won't be able to brush it off.

Jealousy: 1
Me: 1

Maybe we can work together.

4

—⟨∿∿⟩—

RUN INTO SUMMER LIKE

Della and I are drunk at the top of Mont-Royal. We have an
open blue plastic thermos of red wine at our feet. It's the first
day of spring and it's midnight and we've been peeling off
layers of winter all day. We stand facing each other, as if to
exchange vows, chests heaving from racing up the mountain
to the sky. My face is hurting from smiling so much, aching at
the edges of my words. She reaches out to hold my face in her
hands, dirty palms form a bowl to rest my chin. I'm standing
on a tree stump so we are eye to eye. It's hard to stay steady.
I worry I may start to drool or laugh, I feel so unhinged from
my body. It's been one of those days I don't want to end. Our
goal was to shirk all responsibility merely to enjoy the lack

of everyday obligations, to create fullness and purpose out of each other. Our knees are the colour of ground-in grass. Our boots are caked in mud caskets. Under our nails is a mixture of minerals and organic matter, knuckles scraped by tree bark. We are the thaw embodied.

She says, *You have changed me, Eve, you are the single most important person in my life. If you were to leave me, I would die.*

At that moment, our breath circling from my lungs and into hers, I am changed. Perhaps before this I could describe our relationship as an experiment, a happy accident, but this was irrefutable. I was completely consumed and consuming. It was as though we created some sort of object between us that we could see and almost hold. I would risk everything I've ever known to know only this. I wanted to honour her in a way that was understandable to every part of me. It was as though I could distill the meaning of us into something I could pour into a porcelain cup. Our bodies on top of this city, rulers of love.

Originally, we were celebrating the fact that I got into Concordia's visual arts program. But the congratulatory brunch she took me to at Café Santropol had turned into wine, which had turned into a day for declarations. I had a sense of spring in my body, that this season would meld into summer like a running-jump movie kiss. There would be days and days like this. xxxx gone away on a sojourn I didn't care to note the details of, she simply ceased to be. Summer in Montreal in love is almost too much emotion·to hold in an open mouth, it spills over, it causes me to not need any sleep. I don't think I will ever feel as awake as I did in the summer of 1995.

5

⁓

MY CANADA
INCLUDES YOU

OCTOBER 1995

"This referendum, this rendezvous, may be the last one, the last chance you will have to procure for yourselves a country that is truly yours. It is not given to all peoples to have a second chance." Premier Jacques Parizeau, on Quebec television, October 1, 1995.

Montreal remembers, just like the licence plate says. It's a wilting memory, erratic in temperature. The economy in flux like a mis-stickered Rubik's cube. The mouths of most streets are open and prompt us to indulge. Wrought-iron staircases twist around our hearts, strengthening the aortas, tugging. Whatever excess we choose will costume us.

Today I choose a silver dress. Specifically, a vintage floor-length evening gown. I feel like it suits this momentous day in Quebec and Canadian history. I sit on my windowsill, watching. Re-imagining. Fingering the voting card I've folded into a paper monster. Sipping warm broth from a lopsided bowl I made in my ceramics class in CEGEP. I look out at the city like it's my home.

An old camera belonging to my grandmother captures me in front of a car that will later date the photograph. "This is me when I was, uh, nineteen ..." I drink. The cliché of the city in decline is basically that: a boring and repetitive tic of a truth. Overheard. Over-spoken. Rhyming like a hopscotch song. Double Double Dutch. *Montréal, c'est toi ma ville*, indeed, like the television jingle says.

Memory is frozen around the branches of the trees that cluster in a slapdash semicircle around the chipped, green copper statues on Mont-Royal. The hardened men stand valiant in their decline, even though their bodies are spray-painted with anarchy signs from a drunken night with Jenny and a can of Krylon red.

I can see the park from my apartment window on Ave de l'Esplanade. I moved in a few months ago, my mother holding back tears as she stuffed the garbage bags full of clothes into the back of her rusty brown Toyota hatchback. Jenny and I sat in the front seat together like attached twins all the way on Highway 20. Della met us outside the apartment and introduced herself to my mother with a big smile, trying to woo her with charm. My mother spoke with Della like she would any of my friends, and Della made surreptitiously gay comments every five minutes.

"Why don't you just tell her?" She slipped her hands around me and touched the skin on my back softly, while my mother was safely in the bathroom filling my cupboards with bars of Ivory soap and rough, aqua-green hand towels purchased in the mid-eighties.

"I dunno."

Della is very honest with her family about every single detail in her life, even with her grandfather who does not understand lesbianism and called me *the prostitute* when I went over to his house for a family dinner last year. No one mentions her mother, ever, even though there are photos of her all over the house. There are only two topics: politics and gossip. If she arrives hungover, she will say so. Her dad will arrive late from the long drive up from Quebec City, and fall asleep early after several beers. His face will be red. Della will pat his head after he passes out on the couch. They will sit across from one another like mirror images.

The scene from my apartment window is nothing special until someone comes to visit and says, "Wow, quite a view." Now when I give people the tour I say "and I have a fabulous view" like it's an antique trunk or an impressive painting. I live with Rachel, a twenty-five year old writer, master's student and activist who talks really fast and is hardly ever home. My other roommate is called Seven; he keeps his age a secret, like me, and is a long-time friend of Rachel. They dated in high school, even went to prom, and then came out to each other.

I answered an ad posted on a bulletin board at L'Andro-
gyne, the gay bookstore on the Main. *Homo Haven* — *5 1/2,*
cat lover, smoke positive, must like good music. Perfect. I called
from the pay phone at the Second Cup on the corner of Bagg
Street. They asked me my favourite band, I said it was a
toss-up between Team Dresch and Fugazi and they said to
come right away.

I showed up at the apartment for the first time feeling nervous. It was perfect. They led me up the stairs to the second
floor, through a narrow living room and into the kitchen. The
first thing I noticed about Seven was that I recognized him
from the bar where he worked, he poured me doubles instead
of singles and pinched my cheeks. Remember how cute River
Phoenix was in *Running on Empty?* That's basically Seven,
only way gayer and more punk rock. Ten years older than
River in that movie, but you'd never know it from his smooth
face. He was sporting a baby pink Mohawk at the time. A few
face piercings. A red and pink tattoo of a unicorn on his right
bicep. He didn't seem to recognize me back, though. Rachel
wore combat boots, baggy, black army shorts, a T-shirt with
Chainsaw Records on the front, no bra and a plaid shirt,
unbuttoned. She still looked kinda femme though. Her hair
was choppy black and short with little bits of long every so
often and she had those intense hoop earrings that stretched
the holes in her earlobes out to the size of a dime. She had
black eyeliner around her ice-blue eyes, covered in dark-
rimmed glasses and a habit of fiddling with them. I noticed
her hands were wrinkled and boney. If you looked only at her
hands you'd think she was forty. The kitchen table was

covered in books. *The Persistent Desire. Bodies that Matter. Borderlands.*

"My thesis," she explained, giggling nervously and stacking them up where the wall met the table. Seven lit a cigarette and offered me a mug of coffee. The mugs had woman symbols on them. "They're from my work," Rachel said, "at the women's centre. A little cheesy, but you know, perfect for a café au lait." I took a sip and it was too hot, but I pretended it wasn't. I tried to look casual yet interested yet not too intense yet not too spacey. I was entirely too aware of my hands. I drummed my fingers on the table and said, "I love the apartment. I'm not too noisy, I like to party every once in a while but you know, not all the time."

Why did I use "party" as a verb? God. The vernacular of Dorval was going to give me away as very uncool. I stared at the framed poster of a butch/femme couple dancing that was the cover of an Outpunk compilation album. "I have that same poster," I lied, though I had wanted it, had thought about trying to get one.

I liked them both right away. I'm not sure why — I felt drawn to them. My pulse sped up, I began to sweat and blush. I had the feeling I'd know them for a long time, and that there was a reason why I saw the ad and answered right away. Normally I'd procrastinate making such a big decision, but I knew it was right.

They showed me my potential bedroom, one of the two that faced the front of the house, overlooking the street and the park. Seven's was on the right, his door shut tight — *It's a disaster, uh, Eve, right? Eve, yeah, you don't want to see it.*

The empty room was on the left and was perfect. White walls, high ceilings, a beautiful window seat, a closet. It even smelled better than the rest of the apartment, like lavender or cedar. "Our last roommate worked in a candle factory. She always smelled like vanilla and cherry," Rachel explained.

Rachel's room was at the back of the house off the kitchen, like it was supposed to have been a dining room. It was immaculate and smaller than the other two, but so organized. I had the feeling that she could've lived perfectly in an over-head compartment. A loft bed with a desk underneath it, bookshelves on every wall, perfectly in order. An open closet with everything on its hanger, a fold-up ironing board, framed photos and political posters. Shoes lined up against one wall, all shining. "It's a disease," said Seven. "She lets me be messy."

They smiled at me, looked at each other and Rachel said, "Well, this is the true test." She lifted her dark blue bedspread up and cooed softly. Out emerged a fat black-and-white cat looking vaguely annoyed. "This is Gertrude Stein." Gertrude sniffed at my shoes and I leaned down to let her smell my hand and then rubbed her head gently. "Oh my, you're a cute little dumpling." Gertrude rubbed against my legs and then slumped over approvingly to lick her paw.

"You're in," said Rachel, satisfied. Seven nodded and shrugged. "If you want the room, it's yours."

Later, Seven would tell me they'd seen four people that day and they were all a little bit crazy, and they were tired, and I seemed like I was harmless, easy to intimidate, would probably pay the bills on time every month. Maybe I'd just stay for a few months anyway, so why not.

Jenny came over on the first night there to help me unpack. She sat in the window seat smoking and trying on my bras while I pulled stubborn pillowcases onto my pillows, threw my baby quilt over the futon mattress on my floor and manoeuvred it to one corner.

"So, you're like, really gay now, like really a lesbo?"

"I dunno. I still like guys sometimes."

"Hmm. I wish I was a lesbo."

When we were sixteen, Jenny and I, fake IDs in hand, had gone to a gay dance club called KOX in the east end. She made out with three different girls on the dance floor while I stood shy and jealous with a drag queen named Amanda I'd befriended in the bathroom.

"*That bitch*," Amanda said.

I hadn't even kissed a girl yet.

When I asked her how it was she said, "It was cool."

"Like, better than boys?"

"I dunno. Same, I guess."

Her ambivalence was enraging.

Jenny ended up moving two blocks away on Clark above Mont-Royal in a loft with her new boyfriend. She immediately got herself a German Shepherd she named Neneh Cherry. That's how Jenny is. She wouldn't worry about how she was going to take care of a dog, she just took a stray one home on a whim and kept him. We'd been seeing less and less of one another as our social circles grew more disparate along the lines of sexual orientation. She started dating a jock. "Can you believe it, a fucking jock?" she said. "He thinks my tattoos are so bad-ass. It's hilarious." We'd meet up in the park sometimes, hold coffees while walking her dog and catch up.

"So, I started stripping," she said matter-of-factly, as if she'd said she started taking yoga classes.

"Oh my God. Are you serious?"

"Yup." She bit her lip, smiling.

"Is it good money?"

"Yeah. I'm saving up to travel."

"Don't you get shy?"

"No, actually. I was nervous at first, then you get used to it."

"Hmmm. Do you feel, I dunno, exploited?"

"No. It really highlights how dumb guys are."

"Right on." That's not what I meant, really.

"Yeah."

"I just read an anthology for school about strippers in San Francisco trying to unionize."

"Oh yeah? That's fucked. That'll never happen at my bar. Too many bikers running the place."

Jenny seemed to have shed the suburbs from her body like an old, out-of-style dress.

I walked home, kicking the leaves, still feeling kind of surprised at how adult our lives suddenly seemed. I tried to picture Jenny in thigh-high boots and lingerie and I started laughing to myself, wondering if they'd let her wear her fourteen-hole Doc Martins and miniskirt made from an old army surplus T-shirt. I wondered if she's okay, if she's really as tough as she seems. But it made sense too. Guys have been staring at Jenny since she hit puberty. Why not make it lucrative?

I sit on my front steps, pull my skirt down to cover the cold concrete and stare at the people in the park. It feels like a natural extension of my front yard. I've spent countless afternoons there, kissing, smoking, daydreaming. It's become the backdrop for an everyday that will become my history. Stuck on a political and emotional thermometer of memory, I've taken my place at the foot of these statues for the last year, yet I'd never read their accompanying placards. I cannot cite the most nebulous of details, battle dates or statue-worthy escapades.

I am a lazy girl. I will feel it. Taste it. Look at it carefully. But I won't write it down or take a picture. I simply fall in love with archivists. That is how I get things accomplished. Della cuts from every newspaper, pasting text and images in rice paper books. That's appreciation. She is more romantic than this city, and that is something you can't fake.

September started fast with school. New everything. Rachel left to go to the Beijing Women's Conference. Seven got a new lover with a nice apartment so I had the run of the house. I settled in, inviting Della over for dinners I made excitedly, so hyper and energized by my own space, my new independent life in a city so seductive I tried to emulate it with every kiss on Della's neck, every look across the room.

In October, the city seems sad. Seething leaves and greying rivers. Old ghosts knitting sweaters around the perimeter. The summer is like a lover who left too early in the morning without a note, who made you come harder than any other and then ceased to be. The downtown core is covered in graffiti.

The words "Yes" "No" "Oui" "Non" painted across brick and wood. We are plagued with a scattered inability to decide. Chicken or fish? Plaid or stripes? Work or sleep?

Finally able to vote — and this is my vague question.

"Do you agree that ... (Our father who art in ...) Quebec should become sovereign (Do I believe what my mother told me? "Fucking Bill 101!" she yelled at the radio while I was in my car seat.), after having made a formal offer to Canada for a new Economic and Political partnership (Della believes what her father told her. Separation is a victory for the working class. Autonomy is a warm nesting place ... Blah blah blah — light a smoke here, inhale.), within the scope of the Bill respecting the future of Quebec (English people have no rights anymore, said my father, defiantly putting English signs in the window of his store with sloppy paint.) and of the agreement signed on June 12, 1995?"

(Exhale, a stream of smoke, looking heavenward.)

1995 is the year of wallpaper failing. Figures underneath it appearing. Little scraps of forgotten prayers; commercial jingles unknowingly committed to memory. National and Personal identity merging in our sleep.

My friends have been plastering the city with posters urging everyone to spoil their ballots. The posters are green. Neutral. The colour of locker room walls. Della doesn't like my new friends from school. "It's like they think they invented revolution."

Jenny says I have to vote No unless I'm "totally retarded or brainwashed by the girlfriend."

Della was raised in a small town near Quebec City by a

French father and an English mother. Her mother insisted on putting her on a two-hour bus ride every day to get to an English school so she'd have a "hope in hell" of getting out of said town. She showed me photos of her and her brother holding hands on a country dirt road, smiling on their first day of school. They are little dots in a field with no signs of other human life, no houses, just trees and hay.

Her father disagreed but was never one to fight. Only after her mother's death did her father take up separatism like a religious zealot. Della went along for the ride, despite her eventual Concordia arts degree, her fluency in English, her place in both communities. Della never seemed to say much about her mother at all. I didn't press. Della had stories she was comfortable telling, and I'd hear them told again and again at parties, and I'd feel slightly smug that I already knew the endings, the punchlines. She told them with a similar inflection each time. She spun a beautiful sparkling string of yarn.

"Help me poster!" says Dave into my answering machine. He is a sweet, scruffy boy who wears red scarves in winter and reads a lot of leftist political theory. I met him at a screening of *Manufacturing Consent* at Concordia. I don't call him back. Ever. It's another one of my many faults; the phone call unreturned. He always spells out his phone number in a careful, slow monotone, pauses and then says maybe you need to get a pen right now? Okay, it's 555-0994, breathing deep between each number. Something in me must actually like the burning guilt in my gut that arrives when I see him across the street, walking towards me.

Right now he is looking up at me from the street outside my window. I lean my silver body against the glass. He looks away, smiling. I motion him in with an extended curled finger.

Sometimes I kiss Dave when I'm drunk. I'm not sure why. His face is full of longing, and I want to hold it still, all that possibility. I chew his bottom lip and line it with my tongue, laughing. He looks at me very seriously afterwards and I feel bad, like I squished a small animal too hard because it was just too adorable. Like when you want to put a kitten in your mouth because it's excruciatingly cute. He sits at the end of my bed and plays the same Pixies song over and over on my acoustic guitar. He's the kind of friend you don't have to feel bad about having silences with. You can just sit there and be comfortable.

Della only gets jealous when I kiss guys. Girls can come trailing out of my room like daisies on a chain and she won't blink. She won't even say hi to him when we see him. She just stares until he gets really uncomfortable and leaves. He's too apologetic for being a man that he doesn't say anything about her being such an asshole.

The graffiti down the street from my apartment says *Learn French, Wimps*. I think that Dave wrote it. He speaks French with a horrible Toronto private school accent but it doesn't embarrass him.

My aunt Beverly refuses to speak French when she buys cigarettes at my corner store. "Honestly, I don't know how you live in the east end. People are so goddamn fucking rude," Bev says, punctuating her rant by spitting on the ground in front of her red ankle boots. My dad's youngest sister, she's thirty, so is relatively aware of the complexities of my life downtown. She is the only one in my family who knows I'm a dyke. My dad was twenty when I was born, so she's always felt like more of an older sister, and he's always taken care of her like a dad, my grandfather having died when he was a child and my grandmother Annie, a bit of a nutcase by all accounts, when I was eight.

Bev is furious that I am in love with Della, a separatist. She calls her "the separatist." Della calls her "the bitch." When they met, they both smoked furiously (Bev, *Belmont Milds*, Della, *Gauloises*) while I talked ceaselessly. I do that when I'm nervous. Babble about nothing.

I introduced them because I thought they had a lot in common — Della always joked about starting a dead mother's club, to talk about it with other people who understood. I thought Aunt Bev would be a perfect candidate, articulate about loss, honest in a no-bullshit way, just like Della. But it wasn't going to happen. Della tried, but Bev said, "Evie, there's something about her. It's not right. She's not right." She would then elaborate. I tried not to put them in the same room again.

I'm not sure where my opinion lies on Quebec separating. I've been chewing slowly. I can't say I haven't been watching Della watching TV, ripping at her cuticles. She knows what she wants.

Do you ever sit still, in an historic world moment, and think about the size of your hands? The mis-stitch in your sweater sleeve? What you want for dinner? There is something wrong with me.

This morning I woke up in Della's bed, eyes thick with smoky residue, mascara dried against my pale skin. My eyeliner made two black eyes on her white cotton pillow. She was loudly talking on the phone, v-shaped on the couch, wrapped in a pink and green afghan and chain-smoking.

"Make sure you fucking vote, Eric! Don't smoke a fucking joint and fall asleep, you fucking asshole!" The avocado rotary phone was curled in her lap like a cat.

I was late for class and rushed out. Cupping the mouthpiece momentarily, she gave me a raised fist, then blew me a kiss. "It's going to happen, *bébé* — finally, I can feel it!"

Della puts a lot of faith in her premonitions. She dreamt every night this week that she gave birth to Quebec, a tiny baby. Healthy and smiling. It grew and grew until it was like Baby Huey. She laughed in her sleep until she woke herself up in midcackle. When I woke up she was sitting up so tall in the moonlit window. Her presence was daunting.

"I feel her here with us."

"Who?"

"My mother."

I hugged her to me. She started to kiss me hard.

I want to share that moment with her, but the pre-celebratory tequila shots hours earlier drained me of all romantic aspirations. I pushed her back into sleep, promising hot morning sex. Earlier in the night, before licking along a vein of salt, she'd said, "I want you to be mine. All mine." She said it in French but I understood perfectly. And like that, as I felt the booze burn a hole through my core and then warm it up, we tried on a snowsuit of monogamy.

"But we can still kiss people when we're drunk, right?"

"Bien sur!" Like I was even dumb to have asked for that distinction.

I fell asleep thinking, okay, she's mine. All mine. I can be certain. We can contain this, name it, go forward with assurity. xxxx becomes a friend, an ex, no longer the narrator of my most insecure moments.

On the day of the referendum, I get home at noon after a particularily long Intro to Women's Studies class, my answering machine is blinking red with messages from my family. My cousins took free buses from Ottawa to join pro-Canada rallies. My mother insists I should meet them to reconnéct. I watched the news clips of crowds dressed in Canadian regalia as they dropped a big banner of support over a bridge in the West Island. Planting unwanted hickeys all over the news coverage and preaching to the converted. My mother doesn't have any contact with her family, so she really wants me to make sure I stay connected to the cousins on my father's side. She does speak to one older aunt on occasion, who reports every year that the family still unequivocally thinks of her as a sinner whore for running away with my dad at fifteen and leaving the Mennonite way of life.

Aunt Bev calls me to join her at the rally. "Come on! Do it for your country." Her voice is wavering, a sleeve unravelling. "We're going to win! We have to."

I hadn't heard her this passionate about anything since she insisted on keeping me on the phone to watch the entire white Bronco OJ Simpson car chase on CNN or maybe her first year in AA when it was all amends-this and higher-power that.

"I don't really feel passionate about it ... that way ..." Why didn't I just say I had to work?

Her voice is an eggshell breaking, "Oh well, stay home and pray then. We need a strong Canada."

"What does that even mean?"

"Oh Eve, this isn't time for semantics and your 'I'm in College' bullshit."

I'm not sure exactly what I hope will happen. I feel panic. But only because I am sure that I have developed a heart murmur. I can feel it when I move my arms above my head. Whirring. I'm going to drop dead in the voter's booth and the tabloids will eat it up. Maybe if I wear a slutty enough top, I'll make the cover of *'Allo Police*.

My fingers go numb while I paint ice-blue stars on my balcony railing. I dip the thin brush into a mason jar of muddy blue water. I smoke too many cigarettes.

I slip into the delicate silver ankle boots that match my gown. Pull on a wool cardigan and head out towards the Sun Youth building on St-Urbain that's being used as a polling station. I watch my feet as they step along, avoiding the cracks in the sidewalk, old habit. It's like every other day this week, really grey and hazy. A day for depression and headaches where it almost rains and then decides not to.

In the voting booth I notice my boots are scuffed, might need a new coat of silver spray paint. I have what feels like several thousand pieces of ID stuffed in my bra and this makes me scared. I am concerned that everyone seems to be functioning normally — not like today could change the course of my entire life.

I mark an X.

I run home. I don't know why. Do you ever just need to see how fast you can go? I want it to pour. I want something to happen, fast, and I guess I'll have to make that movement myself.

I slam the door of my apartment shut and breathe heavily against it, as if I've been chased. I spend the rest of the afternoon on an art project, ignoring the world outside my room.

After the polls close, I sit on the living room couch, on the phone with my mother. We both keep the CBC news on. Rachel makes a pumpkin pie, cutting herself with the can opener and sucking at the cut as she continues to dish out purée into a yellow plastic bowl. She talks fast because she is nervous, even though I am clearly on the phone. *Won't it be weird, you know, if we separate, I mean, like, will I go to work tomorrow? Will there be a riot? Do you remember the last time we were in a riot and I was on painkillers for my wisdom tooth and I thought it was all a video game? Remember? God, it would be fucking awesome if I didn't have to work tomorrow. Do you want pie? I'm so hungry.*

Within half an hour of the polls closing, "yes" was at fifty-six percent.

That's still only one percent of the vote, explains Rachel.

I nod as though I've also done the math so as not to appear as ignorant about our electoral process as I actually am.

Call-waiting beeps. I say a quick goodbye to my mother. Della's calling from a pay phone. Her voice is a sour glaze.

"*Viens ici, tu me manques*," she says. I get another jolt of excitement about our new-found monogamy. I follow her breathy command, like Ms. Pac-Man chewing up those idiotic white dots.

Rachel rolls her eyes. "I don't know what you see in her."

"She asked me to be monogamous!"

"Really?" Rachel shrugged. "Sounds like it's getting serious."

I didn't like how good it felt that monogamy was somehow legitimizing our relationship, but I did feel reassured. Like it confirmed to the people outside of us what was happening, that we were not just some casual fling, too different in age. I wasn't just some conquest or amusement. I was Della's primary girlfriend. I felt like someone had given me a firm role, a business card, a definite place.

Della is at SKY, a queer bar on Ste-Catherine. I can hardly hear her through the phone, there's so much audible revelry. It sounds exciting. Her voice strings together sentences and laughter.

I get on my bike and peddle south fast in the cold drizzle, the charged air begging for a downpour. My silver dress is almost getting caught in the spokes at every push down of my boot but I don't stop to tie the skirt into a tidy knot at my thigh. I'm a silver pinball bouncing against curbs, averting car doors by fractions of seconds, the yells of angry pedestrians like the high-pitched pings signalling points, speeding through yellow lights, a little out of my head.

I glide down Pine Avenue and turn right onto St-Denis. The streets are pretty empty but the bars look full. I feel like a tourist twisting east. My knuckles are raw from the cold as I chose to keep my outfit uniformly silver, uninterrupted by the usual fingerless gloves. By the time I get to Beaudry I feel deflated, not the confident pinball from the Plateau but a rain-soaked minnow, muddied gills uncertain, gasping for oxygen. I think I might be developing asthma. I push my bike up onto the sidewalk, I lock it up against a post.

I am greeted by a wall of smoke and a crowd as thick as cold butter. I cough immediately even though I've moved up to a deck a day. Definitely asthma. A drag queen, Mado, is wearing a shirt made of glow-sticks and is standing on the bar yelling cheers, revving up the crowd.

I make my way towards Della, who is sitting with her half-smirk, semi-eyelid smile. She kisses me on the mouth, pinches my cheeks, slips a hand under my skirt and up my thigh. I stay quiet, smiling wide.

Della's brother smiles at me and winks, *Salut Eve!* xxxx and her new wife, Isabelle, a quiet butch who used to be my gym teacher in high school, are sitting together like a two-coloured knitted scarf. They greet me with a unified *Hey*. The room is warm and inviting and I don't feel unwelcome at all, even though I definitely feel a little like an imposter, like I have a neon sign across my chest that says SPY.

Della calls Isabelle *xxxx's purse*. She really is quiet, an accessory to xxxx's whimsical personality, but I wonder if that is jealousy talking. I'm pretty sure they're monogamous now, which is a source of both amusement and relief for me.

I give Isabelle some flirty eyes, almost by accident. I'm just so relieved that she exists, a physical barrier between Della and xxxx, that I treat her like an adorable kitten, someone who makes me coo. I don't think she knows what to do with me. Sometimes she looks at me like I caught her stealing, caught her being a big gay lord, like I may just run back to my suburban high school and tell everyone what they already suspect anyway. I remember calling other girls lezzies in grade seven, saying, *You're just like Miss Boucher! Boucher the Bull Dyke.* I can't believe we're across from each other, nothing odd about it.

I try to light a cigarette but my lighter is empty. I click and click nervously, sighing.

"*Cherie,*" says xxxx, reaching out to touch my hand across Isabelle's lap, handing me her Zippo. "I have a dress for you. Long, red. I think you'll like it. It's too small for me." She runs her hands over her D-cups as explanation. I blush. She has recently taken to calling me pet names, like an older sister might. She's also taken to giving me hand-me-downs, offering me cigarettes, and catching my eye whenever a butch says something dumb about girls. *Solidarity,* she'll whisper, and squeeze my hand.

I'm not sure what to do about it, so I mostly just smile. I am definitely over any attraction, working on the heart-seizing jealousy. I've moved up some points. The crowd is really warm, people are excited. I down two pints and feel a part of everything.

"We're Quebeckers!" Eric whispers to me. "You don't have to look so scared, Eve. We disagree and we talk about things, we drink!" He clinks his glass against mine and smiles wide. I take a breathless sip of beer and think, *Fuck the two solitudes bullshit.*

I relax. I start to feel a sense of calm. I look at Della in a swoon. She looks away.

There's something about her demeanour, she can shift so quick. I anticipate it. Now all I can think is: What will she do? What do I have to prepare for?

I ask Della if she wants to walk to the corner store for some snacks so we can be alone for a minute. In French she snaps at me for not being committed to the cause. She hardly ever speaks in French to me since she knows I'm not totally fluent. The energy shifts.

I guess a moment passes, a long moment, it dissolves into my blushing cheeks. I don't want snacks anymore anyway.

She translates slowly, like I'm retarded, and slurs, *I can't be in love with someone who is apolitical*, slamming her beer down on the table like an exclamation point.

"Everyone has a politic. Even not having a politic is a politic," I snap, flicking xxxx's lighter to an open flame, slowly lighting my cigarette to show her comments don't affect me. My cheeks continue to burn, betraying me.

"Besides, you sit at home while I'm out protesting! You don't even call to see if I'm in jail."

"I really don't think Taking Back the Night or picketing the pro-lifers for the fiftieth time is really sticking it to the man, darling. You're just walking around in circles, literally."

People start to stare. I'm definitely the only anglo in the bar. I switch to French.

Mado is yelling something funny, everyone laughs except me because I don't catch the meaning. I fake it with a hearty guffaw that turns into a choking cough. I blush some more.

Isabelle says, in French, "Easy, Della, you've had a lot to drink." I note Isabelle has no discernable accent in French or English.

Jealousy: 10
Me: -10

"That's beside the point, she will never love me right."

Like I'm not even there, like I'm one of the talking heads on the TV. I understand her perfectly, I will never love her right. Della's brother looks like he has no idea what's going on. He watches Mado who is now telling everyone not to give up! But it's clear what the results are going to be. She's telling everyone that it doesn't matter what the results are, we're still us! We'll still be queer tomorrow! The crowd is beginning to look visibly disappointed. I firm my face completely off, betray nothing, my eyes dimming headlights. Nothing is certain yet but it's not looking good for yes.

I get up and turn towards the door. I walk slowly, feigning calm indignance. xxxx follows me through the crowd. She stands in the archway of the door, a hard rain burns me as I unlock my bike. "She's just wasted, and an asshole. I mean, you know how it goes. She's so passionate about Quebec, it's like everyone English is an enemy."

"Whatever," I wipe the seat of my bike with the ends of my skirt. "She's English, too. What about her mom?"

"You can never understand this, Eve. You just can't. You act like it's silly, some cause she's committed to this week."

"No, I don't! I try to understand, I do, intellectually I understand."

"Why haven't you learned to speak French any better than you do? I've heard you speak it, you can do it. You just ..."

"I get shy. I sound stupid."

"Well, she notices. And it's important to her. But the point

I was going to make coming out here is, well, she's an asshole right now. You deserve better, Eve. You're so ..."

"Young?" Maybe if I say it with a smirk she'll note I'm smarter than she thinks I am.

"No, well yeah, but I meant to say ... submissive."

"I'm not submissive!"

"Yes, you let her walk all over you."

"No, no, I don't."

xxxx smiles, gives me an awkward hug. "You deserve better and you should stand up for yourself. But maybe today, tonight, you should realize that you being anglo is hard. It's weird for her. You know, the two solitudes thing."

I want to scream, "But you're from fucking Westmount! My mother could've been your father's secretary! Stop pretending to be some poster girl for the worker's party!"

Instead I say, "What about you and Isabelle? She's English. She teaches gym at my old high school!"

"Yeah, but I don't care. I see both sides. And it's really not an us-against-them thing, for most Quebeckers. Della just gets so ... divisive, about everything in her life. And oh, I've always wanted to ask you this, Isabelle told me it's impossible that you are twenty, how old are you really?"

"I'm nineteen ..."

"Uh huh." xxxx smiles at me, likes she's proud of my deceiving skills.

Or perhaps it's condescending. Another way she talks down to me.

I tug the lock off fast and get on my bike, stare at her body retreating into the bar. I note she's wearing one of those ridiculous baby-sized backpacks. Even though it's made of black rubber it still looks stupid. I begin to peddle home so fast. I feel armless. I press play on my Walkman and hear Kathleen Hanna's voice yelling, "Rebel girl, rebel girl." I stop halfway up the hill, breathing hard and coughing up, lungs failing me. I am completely soaked. A sponge of grey, wet air. Little girl. My Walkman falls out into traffic as I'm speeding ahead, I turn to see it get crushed to its death beneath a bus tire. I yell to no one in particular and swerve into a parked car and lose my balance, press my cold palms against it to steady myself. The crazy man outside the bus station stops talking to himself long enough to stare at me with a questioning look.

I press on ahead and with every stop outside a bar or store the song "Wonderwall" comes out of every speaker. I want to throw rocks at them. I hate that it's our song. It's everyone's song. We're so predictable.

6

FIFTY POINT SIX PERCENT NO/N

Rachel finds me under a fort of wool blankets on the couch, peels back the layers of heavy plaid and off-white. I groan dramatically. She pushes her thick black glasses up her nose and looks at me curiously in a squint, pulling more covers back, revealing my full body splayed in the wet silver dress. She hands me a plate of warm pie awkwardly, which I know is Rachel's way of communicating caring or nurturing; she's like one of those scientist types who can't handle any excess of emotion. We watch the final numbers. I take a bite of pie and it burns the top of my mouth, but I swallow anyway. Everybody looks feverish. Sweaty, half-standing.

Seven emerges from his room in a red cape and booty shorts trimmed with white piping. His shirt says *Fey!*

"Are we going to go riot as a family?" He swoops onto the couch, cuddling up next to me with his legs curled up under him, hands tenderly squeezing my tense shoulders. His warm body is a welcome salve to my numbness. He kisses my cheek and sighs, continues to massage his thumbs into my back, his fingers in the valley between my shoulder blades. My attraction to him is unquestionable and interrupts all essentialist notions I have about my true sexual orientation. Jenny and I were fag hags before we were lesbians. "The fashion is better," she noted when we went to see the Cure shortly after an Indigo Girls concert. It was after that I deduced that I was attracted to girly boys and boyish girls, or girls who later became boys. Boys were always going to be part of the equation.

"What did you vote?" Seven asks, taking his hands away to light a cigarette. I don't answer. Gertrude Stein scratches the sofa leg and meows.

"I voted no, of course, I hope you did, too," Seven says, not really noticing I hadn't answered his question. "I mean, what if it's hard to get drugs over the wall they build? All we'll have is PCP from the bikers and weak granny weed. That's just not healthy. We need easy flow between BC and Quebec to avoid calamity."

Rachel snorts. "Seven ..." Rachel is critical of anyone who doesn't get involved in the issues, read the paper, keep up-to-date on things. But she doesn't expect much from Seven. She allows him to live in his circle of delusion, as she's dubbed it.

"I voted no." Rachel announces. "I feel somewhat uncomfortable about it."

Rachel always speaks about politics like she's giving a media interview. She won't just say she feels kinda fucked-up about it, she's "somewhat uncomfortable."

All week we've been privy to her debates. Her anti-oppression-based politics called into question in the voting booth, because should she not ally herself with the independence of an oppressed group? Should she not support the workers? She threw a mug against the wall a few weeks ago and yelled, *Everyone's a power-hungry, money-grubbing motherfucker, no one deserves to win anything!*

Rachel's parents are English, from the Eastern Townships. Her family had lived there on the same farm for over a hundred years. Every year English kids left for other cities across Canada to go to school. Only a handful returned to farming. Even with all that emotional investment, no one could survive, let alone thrive.

"Why?" I asked. I was pretty sure she was going to vote yes last time we discussed it.

Rachel paused. "I was going to vote yes. I really was. I want it to happen if it's going to happen, but ..."

I expected her to say I just don't want things to change, I want to stay in Canada, I don't want any chaos.

"But they refused to meet with Native leaders about the future of Quebec, they refused to meet with leaders of the immigrant communities, they just didn't seem to have much of a strategy for what would happen after yes came through ..."

"But, essentially you believe in separatism."

"I believe in sovereignty, Eve. There's a big difference for me." Rachel leaned back in her chair with her arms behind her head, her tiny arms looking even smaller than usual. Her unharnessed boobs trying to poke through her thin, grey 7-Year Bitch T-shirt like little nails.

We turn to an audible commotion on the black and white TV. The votes are in. No is confirmed — barely. I finally feel something: relief. This strange and solemn sense of calm that nothing will change. Echoed in my mother's voice on the phone immediately after it's confirmed. "Thank God."

How can anything really be that close?

I think about my single X, the one I was sure wouldn't matter all that much in the big picture.

One of Seven's lovers arrives at the door, greeted by a sense of anticlimax and uncertainty engulfed by our three bodies in the living room. He is wearing so much CK One cologne I can hardly breathe. We disperse into our rooms. I sit in my window seat, the only sound is the pulsing house music from Seven's room vibrating the walls, making me feel shaky. I chain-smoke and drink tea, watch for any sign of upheaval on the streets. It's distinctly quiet when I go to the corner store at St-Urbain to buy more smokes, try to sweet-talk my way into buying a single can of beer even though it's after 11:00 p.m. It works. The store owner thinks Della is a little boy. Every time she comes in with me to buy groceries he acts like she's such a cute kid buying eggs for her big sister in the morning. It's hilarious. I look into the faces of people walking their dogs, standing on their stoops, wondering what 50.6 percent *no* and 49.4 percent *yes* looks like. Looks like the same thing. No one east of Atwater Street has the guts to look relieved.

Just as I'm settling into bed, feeling uneasy about my sense of relief, the doorbell rings. I know it's Della so I don't answer it. She presses her finger to the worn-in rectangular pad, further smudging the markered arrow directing visitors to the upper level. Again and again. I pull my pink flannel sheets up over my head and groan. My heart is pounding, because I am happy she's come to me. But my brain is telling me I shouldn't be so excited. That I should be mad.

If xxxx wasn't with Isabelle, would she have even bothered coming by? Is Isabelle the only reason we are still somewhat together? I turn up the No Means No on my little black ghetto blaster by the bed. It distorts.

Rachel appears at my door. "I was knocking but I guess you didn't hear me!" she yells, peeking her head around the corner. She's wearing flannel PJ bottoms and an old Smiths T-shirt. I turn down the volume knob on the ghetto blaster next to my mattress. She walks across my room to look out the front window and turns to face me with her eyebrows raised in points. I note her hair is starting to dread a little from lack of care, some parts have grown out, a mass of cut curls of different lengths. She clicks her tongue against the top of her mouth, exhaling sharply then groaning. "It's her. What's her fucking problem?" She kneels down on the window seat and turns to look at me.

I shrug, sitting up. "Sorry, dude."

"I should really introduce you to some cooler chicks."

Before Rachel can verbally run through her rolodex of available single queer girls, as she does every time Della "pulls some bullshit," we are interrupted by the sparkle crash of breaking glass. I run to the door at the top of the stairs, unlock the chain-link and peer around the corner purposefully, suddenly worried that Della split right before the appearance of a deranged psychopath. I walk halfway down the enclosed staircase tentatively, grabbing onto the rubber mallet we keep by the door in case of a break-in. I want to yell that the only thing we have of value is four copies of the same Everything But The Girl CD and a VCR from 1987. The VCR has a soul and refuses to record *X-Files* episodes.

But it *is* her.

She has punched in one of the quarter-square panes in the window of the front door.

I slip on my flip-flop sandals, cold and abandoned on the stairs from last summer, grab the broom leaning against the stairwell wall, and run down. When I open the door and the cold rushes in, Della tries unsuccessfully to hide her bleeding fist. It looks like a ripped-up bloodied hibiscus.

I don't say anything after her muttered string of apologies. I just turn and walk upstairs, hearing her guilt-heavy steps behind mine.

I sweep up the glass and tape up a garbage bag over the hole while Rachel wraps Della's fist in a clean towel. Della sits on the couch and Rachel sits in the armchair and they glare uncomfortably at each other. The ugly, green wood coffee table acts as a pacifying object. The bleeding slows, stops. We don't say anything. I busy myself cleaning the dishes off the coffee table, wiping down drips of pie filling and old coffee rings on the wood. It's been days since anyone ran a cloth over the table, I'm not sure why it's suddenly imperative that I do this.

On television Jacques Parizeau approaches the microphone. "We have lost, but not by much."

Rachel says, "Go to Hotel Dieu," mostly, I suspect, because she wants Della to leave. She snaps her gum, leaning over in the red armchair with her elbows on her knees and her head in her hands, tapping her fingers against her cheeks, defiant. I love her for this uncomplicated display of certainty. She stares at Della hard, willing her to take some responsibility. Was she trying to be my older sister or was she simply annoyed at constantly having to deal with her in the house? I felt ashamed at my weakness yet devastated at the idea of Della leaving.

"*Non, c'est correcte*," Della says, looking at Rachel out of the corner of her eye, vaguely sheepish but too drunk and reticent to put forth a certain air of apology.

We all turn to the TV as Parizeau commits political suicide. "It's true that we have been beaten. In essence, by what? By money, by the ethnic vote, essentially. And so ..."

Rachel gasps, laughing. *What the fuck did he say?* She grabs her scruffy hair in both hands, eyebrows raised in disbelief.

"He's crushed. It's the weight of failure," Della offers.

"You understand being a racist prick?" I say, before I can stop myself.

Rachel smiles at me. "Yeah. Exactly."

Della stands suddenly, braces herself against the wall behind the couch. I feel slightly smug that I may have said something Rachel found insightful.

"I'm just saying, I understand being crushed by failure. This is a big deal, you know. You are all just casual observers, but —"

"How can you say we're impassive, Della? I've thought of nothing else for weeks. You don't own the emotional weight of the referendum." Rachel is standing now, facing her, like two lions or gargoyles in a faceoff of belief and position.

Della mumbles, "*Tu sais ce que je vais dire ...*" before swerving down the hallway towards my bedroom, pushing open my door with an open palm, and crawling under my blankets like a punished child.

I walk in and close the door before whispering, "I should ask you to leave. If I had any sense I'd tell you to fuck off."

"If you had any sense you'd have told me that a year ago," emerges from under the blankets like a comic book dialogue bubble.

"You're going to have to pay for the window."

"Tell your landlord someone broke in. He'll have insurance."

You're so submissive echoes in my head.

"You're going to have to pay for the window."

Nothing.

"I'm serious. You have. To. Pay. For. It."

"Okay."

I lie down on top of the blankets and hug her shape to sleep, a cocktail of emotions. I say, *I love you like nothing else matters.* I go to sleep thinking what a stupid thing to say. *Like nothing else matters.* It repeats in my head in a loop and I want to say something else, but she is asleep, and I have become a dumb romantic.

I go into the living room and set up shop on the couch, reading until Seven arrives back home carrying giant plastic bags overflowing with costume materials. Tomorrow it will be Halloween and no one seems to care except Seven. He will dress like JoJo, the over-the-top blond drag queen-esque spokeswoman for *JoJo's Psychic Alliance*, and I'm going to be the little poodle she carries around like a purse. We will go out dancing. "It's important to remember, dear Evie, that Halloween is a queer spiritual holiday," Seven says, pouring two shots of Jägermeister into shot glasses shaped like skulls. When I suggest we are too old to really indulge in much beyond handing out candy, he looks exasperated.

"You have so much to learn about being a good homo," he says before leaning in to suck on my neck and give me a hickey. "Now, this will make her jealous. When she asks you who gave it to you, just shrug."

I touch my hand to my neck to feel the slimy hot mark. "Seven, what did you really vote?" I suspected that he voted yes, that his last answer had been posturing, that he was still loyal to how he was raised.

"I voted no," he says quickly with an unapologetic shrug, before downing the shot of dark green herbal sludge.

"Why?"

"It's not my revolution. It's not going to change anything for queers. It might even make everything worse. Plus, it would make my dad too happy, and we can't have that."

"No, we can't have that," I say, cheersing the air before doing my shot. "Seven, have you ever been in love?"

"Sure. Tons of times. Every Friday night at the bathhouse."

"No, like real love, like The One. Like the person you'd take a bullet for."

"Eve, you're so dramatic! That kind of love is a fiction."

7

BUNCH OF
FUCKING FEMINISTS

DECEMBER 1995

November passes in a blur of collective meetings at the women's centre at Concordia, where I've decided to focus my energy on something positive. Rachel has taken me under her wing. We bike to meetings together, gossip at home about the collective members, spend lots of time at the photocopy place making stickers and posters for our campaigns. Our latest ones say *You're Beautiful!* in big letters with *It's society that's fucked up* in a smaller font underneath. We stick them on bathroom mirrors all over school and in restaurants.

Between meetings, work and first-semester classes, I take bags of trail mix and my textbooks to the scratchy blue couch of the women's centre. Flanked by shelves of feminist books and magazines, interrupted only by the occasional political debate or gossip session, I find myself calming down. I don't wait for phone calls. I'm not always available for Della. I pour my heart into what really matters — this roughly translates into overthrowing cock rock and ending violence against women. Shaving my head and reading bell hooks, Minnie Bruce Pratt, Sarah Schulman, Cindy Patton.

"*Inventing* AIDS?" Della picks up the tattered purple paperback I'm reading on the steps outside the centre, where I've been gathering up some sun, taking notes and increasing my addiction to coffee and cigarettes. She runs another hand over my newly shaven head.

"Yeah, it's for my class on women and HIV."

"Oh yeah, Denise is the TA right?"

Why must every dyke over the age of twenty-five know each other?

"Yeah."

"I used to date her."

"Oh yeah."

"She told me you were in her class when I ran into her the other day."

"Yeah." There is no such thing as privacy or teacher-crushes existing in a vacuum. Now every time I write a paper I'm going to picture her and Della doing it.

"Did she say I was smart?"

"She said you were cute, part of this little enclave of eager newbie queers. Very *earnest.*"

Great. Cute. Earnest. My favourite things to be. Next class I'll wear a giant pink bow in my hair, if I had hair.

"Are you coming to the action tonight?" I'm part of an organizing committee to memorialize the December 6 massacre.

We're going to stop traffic on Ste-Catherine Street for fourteen minutes, one minute for each woman killed by Marc Lepine at École Polytechnique in 1989.

"I'm going to try, bébé. I have a painting I'm working on, I'm really into it."

I nod.

She nods.

We make out like mad until the kids upstairs at the gay and lesbian student group start clapping and yelling, "Ten percent is not enough! Recruit! Recruit! Recruit!" Della gives them the finger.

Shortly after sundown, I'm holding a giant orange megaphone in the middle of rush hour traffic. Pedestrians are swearing. I start nervously saying each name while other women hand out stickers and pamphlets, and most gather in a tight circle around the intersection holding hands and candles. Traffic backs up for blocks and no cops arrive. I expected them to come immediately. I have a lawyer's number scrawled on my arm and my fingers are frozen, but my heart is full and pounding. I close my eyes, remembering watching the news in grade eight while my mother sat white with horror and shock, trying to explain the significance of what had occurred. To me, it seemed like another freak occurrence of random violence. *This was not random*, she explained.

As I call the last name, and see some police on horseback approaching through the crowds, my heart races. I remember Della's baton scars and Jenny being dragged away, and I will myself to stay still and pay tribute properly. Some women are crying, some are looking solemn, others smiling slightly with pride that we'd pulled the action off. Jenny holds Melanie's hand and they both look at me encouragingly. I laugh to myself that I told Jenny to wear something practical and she arrived in stiletto boots and a fuzzy fake leopard-fur coat. When we disperse, I walk away from the crowd by myself, trying to feign nonchalance, like I'm just some chick carrying a megaphone through the streets. It's an awkward transition from feeling so insulated by the crowd to my solitary pair of legs. My limbs feel weightless, floating, mechanical.

We've arranged to meet at the bar where a girl band from Toronto will be playing and some poets, including Rachel, will be reading. We're charging a sliding scale admission, giving all the profits to a local women's shelter. I volunteered to work the door and when I get there Melanie greets me with a thermos filled with whiskey and Coke and a *Good job*.

Rachel's poetry silences the room. Even the drunk guys at the back who have no idea what's going on with all the gay lords stop to listen. I watch her and my heart swells with pride and the knowledge that I am lucky to know her.

Della arrives halfway though the night. I watch her through the glass door of the club from my post at the door where I'm stamping hands with a flourish. She smokes a cigarette, as if she knows she's being watched. When she pushes through the doors, she leans in to kiss me. I note we are both totally wasted. "Great turnout," she says in my ear before taking my earlobe in between her teeth gently. "Great job. Sorry I missed the action. I saw it on the news, though. You looked hot. Let me buy you a drink."

Since the referendum Della has turned into a moody drunken uncle. Boozy, inappropriate and forgetful. The only thing she does — besides berate, drink and rant — is paint. If I want to see her, I have to go to her apartment, where she's turned the living room into a studio. She started to paint these giant canvas recreations of me. Close-ups of my face while I sleep. An oil painting of Jenny and I at the front of a demonstration against police brutality, perfectly capturing our collective anger and energy. Jenny is wearing a T-shirt that says *Help the M.U.C. Police, Beat Yourself Up*. Della paints her in such brilliant detail, ripped fishnets under a short camouflage skirt, baby-pink army boots, her diamond labret piercing, the arch of her eyebrows. She paints me looking at Jenny adoringly. It's perfect.

The paintings make me feel like a celebrity. She's talking about having another gallery show again. It makes up for the fact that she rarely listens to me or asks me how I am. She's paying such close attention to the lines in my face and the emotion in my eyes. I forgive her her artistic temperament. I trade my second semester Ceramics class for a second-level French. I conjugate verbs thinking of her. We manage monogamy well. *Je vous pardonne, nous pardonne, nos coeurs son lourds.*

I worry about her, the way she is not eating much, only working. After sex, she jumps up to sketch. Her eyes are wild and unruly. It's both attractive and disquieting.

A little mosh pit forms in front of the band and a few girls take their shirts off. Melanie is kissing a shirtless girl with a green mohawk. Jenny's jock boyfriend arrives to find her locking lips with a butchy dyke in a tie. He looks terrified and uncomfortable so Della puts her arm around him and buys him a shot. Her charm could solve wars. He looks like he might want to marry her. At the end of the night he stands so close to my face and says, "Your life is fascinating, Eve, fucking incredible. Everyone is so honest." I have a brief flash of him coming out in three months, but then watch as he grabs Jenny's ass and topples her into a street-side snowbank to make out and think otherwise.

xxxx and Isabelle came to the action, though only xxxx appears at the bar, glued to Della's side. She's not so friendly. As if on cue, she selects the hot lead singer of the band from Toronto as her prey and by last call is sitting on her lap. The singer looks amused. I feel like saying, yes, xxxx, we all know you could get anyone you want in the room, even the singer from the band who's rumoured to have slept with Patti Smith. We get it. Her casual confident beauty looks like something else entirely close up and drunk.

When xxxx slips into the bathroom with the singer, Della rolls her eyes at me and goes outside to smoke joints with Jenny and the Jock. I'm trying to sober up, clutching the tin box of cash from the door sales, making sure I keep everything together when I'm talking to Rachel, making sure she knows she can count on me to get things done. Rachel pinches my cheeks. When will people stop doing that? I stand outside trying to hail a cab, watching Rachel bike away. One comes along and xxxx and band girl run up and jump into it, oblivious that we'd been waiting. Della watches them stumble into the cab. I try to detect a bad mood or a jealous intonation to her words, but she is either adept at not showing it or really doesn't care. She seems concerned with getting me unclothed as soon as possible. Della says she doesn't get jealous. I tell her this has to be a lie. She laughs every time.

Towards the end of December I go home for a few days to study. I stretch out on the basement couch with my books. My aunt, who has moved into the basement after getting evicted, comes home from work and stares at me highlighting and typing away on typewriter. "Stay in school, baby. And watch how much you drink." Then she goes upstairs to drink beer with my parents, until my mom escorts her into my old room, tucking her in, before starting into a marathon conversation with my dad about how to save his sister from ruin.

I sleep on the couch like a guest and feel okay about it, my head filled with memorized quotes and theories. I hope I'll remember the details.

To celebrate after my last exam, I go back to my apartment with clean laundry and a full day ahead of me, spread out with so much promise. I go to the store and buy a bouquet of daisies, bags of assorted fruit, chocolate cake, and a small Christmas tree for Della's apartment.

When I get home there's a message on my machine.

"Hey Eve, it's Della. Listen, I'm spending the day with my grandfather. It's the anniversary of my mother's death and we always spend it together." She exhales into the recording, pauses. "I really miss you though, baby. I hope to see you later tonight. Maybe you could come by? I dunno. I'll call. Maybe I'll meet you at the Metro if it's really late. Okay, I love you."

I look around my apartment at the things I'd planned, hearing her sad resignation from the message in my head. I decide to surprise her by making her apartment look festive and comfortable, a warm hug to come home to after a hard day. I plan every present carefully, making sure the night will pass slowly and soft. As I move around with the details, holding them in my mouth contemplatively, I realize that this is what everyone talks about. The feeling of really being together, beyond the sex, jealousy, drama, intrigue and romance. Real nurturing, bringing comfort to someone, intimacy. I used to regard it all with suspicion, like empty Valentine's Day rituals, the fakery of marriage. But, anticipating her surprise, making her dinner, I feel the newness of longevity and permanence.

I gather the tree and presents into a cab and feel a bubble of excitement to see her face when she arrives home.

Unlocking her door with my new key, worn around my neck, attached to a length of dog chain from the hardware store, what I feel can only be described as a quick incision between my seventh and eight rib without warning. Then several quick kisses with a staple gun to my gumline, emotionally speaking. A sock in the teeth for good measure.

It is somewhat satisfying that xxxx's face turns inside out and monstrous while experiencing an orgasm. The tree lands on the floor with some finality, the dirt falls on my boots. I kick it across the hall. I bury my heart under the floorboards before I walk away.

8

HIGH SCORE — 1995

Jealousy: 50,000,000,000

Me: 0

Merry fucking Christmas.

9

DON'T CHA THINK?

The breakup was inevitable and not like I expected it to be, a triumphant walking away, my own parade. I really thought it would be my decision, slow realizations adding up and moving on, growing up, shedding the skin of this first love bliss. Though it was ultimately my body that packed my things and walked away. Della didn't offer much more than a boyish shrug as explanation. In fact all she said was, "It's your decision, Eve, do what's right for you. I'll support you. I don't want you to go, of course." I felt robbed of my leading-lady moment. Everywhere I go Alanis Morrisette asks me if it's ironic. I throw my radio out the bathroom window, watching it splinter onto the courtyard behind my building.

Della has called every day so far this week. She's ordered drugs from Seven, and shows up when she knows I'll be home.

I hide in my room. Seven tells her I'm entertaining someone, with a wink. Really I'm pressed up against the door, listening to every word.

Today is her third visit for pot. Apparently she's become chronic. Or she's trying to run into me. I walk through the living room in a red negligee, obvious pragmatic study attire, pretending I don't know she is sitting at the coffee table while Seven weighs her wares. I fake surprise with aplomb. My nipples float just beneath the shoreline of the plunging neckline. My mouth betrays hostility. My feet are bare. Seven is pretending to be an oblivious fag, but I know he knows. She knows he knows. He sings along with the music blaring from his room.

"Eve, I was hoping to run into you." She stands in that way that used to get to me, half James Dean, half goofy Robert Smith. She's wearing a Vision Streetwear shirt with long sleeves, chewing on her lip ring. I hate that she can be so honest like that, just admit she was wanting to see me.

"Yeah?" I roll my eyes, keep walking towards the kitchen, rooting through the freezer for some coffee beans. She follows me.

"Eve, I want to apologize."

I close the freezer door, unzip a plastic freezer bag and plunge my hand into the cold coffee beans. I let them sift through my fingers, willing myself to say something mean or pointed or smart.

"I was sad about my mother ..." Della goes into a convoluted story about how xxxx dropped by at the right time, manages to tell me everything without taking an ounce of responsibility.

I turn my back to her, pour the cold beans into the grinder and press down. After a few minutes of grinding noise, I feel her leave the kitchen. The coffee is a fine, useless powder. I didn't want it anyway.

Seven holds me while I dissolve into manic tears. Then he calls to tell her he'll make a house call next time and not to come by again until things are cool. He tells me just to wait a month, one month. By that time things will feel better, he promises. Thirty days, thirty days.

My aunt Bev stops by with cans of beer in a paper bag and we sit on the front step wrapped in blankets with our toques pulled down over our ears, smoking in thick black gloves. She tells me about every guy who ever broke her heart. She's candid and articulate, never dismissive. I feel so thankful for her. I don't ask her why she's drinking again, I decide to not be one of the Program People she talks about negatively when she's not one of them.

When she meets Seven she gives him a big hug and asks him questions about how he knew he was gay, how he feels about women, how he pictures his life at seventy. Seven brings out a bong and she giggles like a little kid. "Fuck, I haven't smoked pot in years!" After inhaling deeply and letting out more laughter she starts in with, "What role do drugs play in your life? How do you feel about selling them? Is it part of your spirituality?" I feel embarrassed, like she's invading his privacy, but when she leaves he tells me he wants to marry her.

Rachel and Seven plan their Christmas celebrations. Every year they host a "homo-hobo" party — for everyone estranged from their families, who have to work or can't afford to travel home. Rachel shoves recipes in my face every five seconds and I help her bake cookies. She notes I am somewhat catatonic.

"I don't know. I guess this is my first broken heart."

Rachel snorts. "It's hard, isn't it? My first girlfriend did a number on me."

"It's hard to imagine anyone holding your attention long enough to break your heart."

"Why do you think I'm like this? I'm totally not over her, really. She shattered me." Rachel using dramatic words like *shattered* took me off guard.

"Where is she now? How did you meet her?"

"We met my first week in Montreal at school. She was my teacher at McGill."

"No!"

"Yup. We had to keep it hidden from everyone at school, plus we were both closeted. In retrospect I can't believe we even lasted as long as we did."

"How long?"

"Three years. Until I was twenty-one. I basically didn't make any friends, just kind of orbited around her, waiting around for her. She was everything. It was incredible, that feeling like everything important was all in one person."

"And now you're a heartbreaker."

"Yeah, yeah. As if."

She stirred the vegan chocolate cake batter, smushing in a frozen banana with a potato masher, looking up at me with a smirk. "You don't realize this now, but Della is so mediocre compared to you. Her arrogance is astounding. She can't keep a job, she ..." Rachel lists off dozens of reasons why Della is a loser and I should be thankful to let her go. I nod vehemently, wanting to believe it. But I don't. I feel like someone took one of my lungs away. I feel like Della was my life-changer and now she is suddenly gone.

I look at Rachel and see she's got a bit of a boyish side, the way she moves around the kitchen. "Do you consider yourself a butch, Rachel?"

She laughs. "No."

"Femme?"

"Hell, no. I'm nothing. I'm queer. I like the ladies. I guess I'm a little of both. Now Seven, Seven's a high femme for sure. Jesus. Sometimes I think he wishes he was a lesbian just for the clothes."

"What do you think I am?"

"Oh God, Eve, are you serious?" she lowers the electric mixer into the plastic bowl, shakes her head like she can't believe me, while the sound drowns out what she's saying. She clicks off a beater dripping with batter and hands it to me. "Such a femme. You're like a baby princess waiting for her first set of false eyelashes to be passed down to her. You smell like a cupcake. You could wear combat boots and a plaid shirt and still be a girl from a hundred yards away."

I laugh, licking the beater, pulling a wooden stool up to the counter, watching as she formed the question "Yeah, but is it just about fashion?"

"I don't know. Be who you want to be, Eve. That's just what I see. I have no idea."

"Femme." I mouth it to myself, giggling. "Okay." For some reason this sounded good, like it fit more than any other moniker hoisted on me like queer, lesbian, bi, whatever. None of those felt right. Femme. Okay, that works.

Before I went home for Christmas, Rachel handed me a sparkling purple gift bag. In it was a copy of *S/he* by Minnie Bruce Pratt, pink sparkling eyeshadow, a seven-inch record by Slant Six called *Ladybug Superfly*. On the card it said, "Here's some femme essentials from your gender retarded roommate, xo Rachel."

I bought her *The Complete Hothead Paisan, Homicidal Lesbian Terrorist* by Diane DiMassa. She squealed like a little girl when she unwrapped it.

On December 23 my father knocks on the door and I try to pretend things are okay. He stands awkwardly in our living room while I go into Seven's room to kiss him on the forehead while he sleeps, leaving him silver and gold glitter nail polish wrapped in magazine paper beside his alarm clock that blinks the wrong time. My dad examines the bookshelves in the living room and suggests a way to make them more sturdy before I hand him a bag of laundry to take down to the car.

I pile into the back seat of the Toyota hatchback with garbage bags of laundry and some half-assed Christmas collages still drying in my lap. We listen to a seventies rock station in silence. The panes of the grey industrial landscape of the Turcotte Yards, the factories leading up to Lachine blend into one unpalatable painting of heartbroken misery.

My mother greets me with, "You look emaciated," and, "What happened to your hair?" and I say, "Merry Christmas."

I help my dad at the store on Christmas Eve, selling guitars to procrastinating fathers who hope their kid will be the next Stevie Ray Vaughan or Jean LeLoup. He says, "You're even crankier with the customers than usual." As always, some guy is playing the introduction to "One" by Metallica on the expensive Fender. My father smiles weakly, encouraging everyone to be creative, but I can tell he's annoyed. "At least it's not 'Stairway to Heaven,'" I note and he laughs. It only takes a few minutes for someone to start humming about a lady who knows from an acoustic one aisle over.

My aunt and I get drunk on a bottle of wine and dye our hair in the basement living room while my parents and their friends sing Christmas carols in four-part harmony upstairs. I tell her I love that she's drinking again, but then regret it. My aunt targets her grey hair, teaches me how to buff my nails and I try to get her to stop ashing into the black-dye-filled Tupperware container. It's strange to see her living there, all of my things now in boxes under the bed. I feel like she's an excellent buffer, an older sister I always wanted. Now that we're both adults, she doesn't treat me like I'm ten.

After a few drinks she says, "Why don't you just tell them you're a big homo?"

"Well, I'm not dating anyone now, so what does it matter?"

"You're heartbroken, eh?"

"Yeah."

The thing with my mother being an ex-Mennonite is that sometimes she's still the hippie radical she wants to be, but keeps some conservative ideas tucked away that come out at strange moments. Like the time we saw a drag queen walking along Ste-Catherine when we were going to a bookstore when I was about ten. I'll never forget the way she said, "Sick, that's just not right."

I tell Bev that I've been sneaking out to the back porch every half hour to burst into tears and then checking my voice mail on the hour in case she calls to say Merry Christmas. I know her and xxxx are drunk at Foufounes Electrique for the punk rock Fuck Christmas party. And I know that, like monogamy, Christmas is a capitalist plot not to be indulged in. I suspect they'll drop by xxxx's parents' mansion around midnight once they are drunk and they can score some great food when they get back from Mass, maybe even envelopes of cash.

"Fuck her!" my aunt says, toasting me with her glass of wine.

"Yeah, fuck her!"

"You know what this is, Eve? Your first adult Christmas. I'll let you in on a secret ... Christmas sucks for everyone but children."

"Yeah, it totally does."

"Just force yourself through this, you'll find someone new in no time. In fact! There's this girl in my improv dance class, she's gay. She's cute too!"

Why must every straight person in my life try to fix me up with the other gay person they know? I picture a waify femme in bad leotards. "No thanks. I'm thinking of going back to men."

We pull the couch out into a bed and I climb in. I keep one hand cupped around the cordless phone. I feel suddenly apart from adolescence, like I'm a guest in their house. I'm aware with certainty at this moment, that I was cared for well as a kid, that I was lucky, and am lucky, to know what it's like to be cared for.

I remember Seven talking about his father's work boots on his back like an iron branding, Rachel's rocky two conversations a year with her parents. I feel aware that I should come out to them, that they deserve the benefit of the doubt at least.

I wake up with this thought pushed forward, procrastinating the inevitable, eating the turkey-free stuffing my mother made especially for me. I open presents, a sweater, a box of chocolates, some guitar strings and a book of short stories. I spend the day in front of the TV in the quiet basement, watching old tapes of *Kids in the Hall*. I feel well loved and lucky, and devastated by a loss I've never known.

Boxing week I work at my dad's store every day, all day. I drown my sorrows in monotony, polish instruments, try to organize the books and clean the storage room. My dad is amazed but doesn't try to stop me. By the thirtieth, I'm ready to leave the suburbs and get back to real life, the sidewalks and bustle, the proximity and urgency of my real urban life.

On New Year's Eve, Melanie and I go to a big warehouse party called Kitty Kitty put on by a dyke about town. Rachel is DJing, we know some girls from around, but no one too intimately. We share a bottle of gin before getting there, wear slinky black dresses and heeled boots. I've stopped being devastated and started being flirty and available. The night is charged. We have too many expectations for the Best Night Ever.

Rachel is looking really hot in a Chainsaw Records T-shirt, her hair all messy and newly blond, mixing a 7-Year Bitch song with novelty group Cunts with Attitude. Seven is dressed in full drag, except he's grown a little beard and wears a mohawk instead of a wig. He's attached by a chain to a hunky shirtless boy in a ball cap and a pair of overalls. He embraces Melanie and me, which results in an accidental hug with the overall boy who smiles politely. He takes us to the bar, buys us four shots of something fruity and disappears as quickly as he came.

Melanie locates her crush and then decides to hang on my arm and make sure she's always at least ten feet away from the crush. This makes cruising impossible. But I don't want anyone anyway, I only want Della. Absence and indifference, I was learning, were hotter than any cologne or pheromone. Show me I'm unimportant or replaceable and I'll lay down in the street for you.

By 3:00 a.m. I am puking into a snowbank. By four, writing devastating nihilistic poetry in the bathroom only to emerge from said room to see xxxx and Della waiting in line. I arch my back, walk confidently by, ignoring their hello nods.

I join Melanie on the dance floor. Before I really know what I'm doing I've grabbed her, whispering to her to *just go with it, okay?* We have an awkward but believable make out. I grab her by the back of her neck theatrically while we kiss sloppily without real desire, except the desire to perform for everyone. There are hollers and claps.

Later, Melanie and I are smoking on the long wooden balcony. Della walks straight up to me, bold and bolder, just like she had the first time we met at the art show. She puts her hands on my face and says, "I've never loved anyone like you."

I see three of her faces and her words make my core sparkle like Pop Rocks candy, but I know enough to censor. To smirk. To walk away, grabbing Melanie's hand, throwing our smokes over the side of the roof and curling back through the window that leads outside. Gathering my coat from the coat-room I saw Isabelle and xxxx in an embrace. I thought about turning around, but forced myself not to. I thought about the things I could yell.

Reaching the clogged artery that is the front door where drunks try to match feet and corresponding boots with a definite lack of finesse, I felt hands on my back, squeezing. Della. "Baby, are you with Melanie now? What the fuck?" she whispered. I didn't expect her to be that dumb. To fall for such an obvious ploy. Maybe she was just taking the bait. I didn't turn around. I kept walking, pulled by Melanie's indignant mittened hand.

Della wasn't wearing a coat or shoes. I went outside, leaving her in the doorway and didn't even bother trying to hail a cab, just teetered away with Melanie on my arm, discussing how girls will always fail us.

We laughed at each other, fell asleep on my living room floor, keys in the front door, our belongings trailing up to the apartment.

"1996!" I said at 7:00 a.m. before throwing up my dinner of Fairmount bagels into the bathroom sink.

"Fucking right!" I hear Seven say from the other room, as Rachel kicks a one-night stand out the door. We've never looked so pale and dehydrated.

Rachel pours water into four purple plastic cups and serves them to us, forming our weakened hands around our own cup. She smiles.

"It's the Chinese Year of the Fire Rat. There's supposed to be a lot of natural disasters."

I make no resolutions.

Rachel lines us all up on the couch and takes a photo, laughing. Somehow, she never looks undone — even when she drinks the most.

10

—◊◊◊—

T-CELL GIANT

Seven is trying to erase his short-term memory.

He swears this to me over cherry pie breakfast at Futenbulle
Diner on Bernard. I'm eating off of his plate with my hands.
We are beginning to feel the winter subside and the thaw
creep into our hearts. Squishing each finger into the
sugary mess of cherry filling and drawing tiny brains on the
scratched white ceramic surface, I'm trying to have one day
without thinking about the breakup. The thirty-day promise
didn't work out so well. Now, at almost ninety days, the pain
was starting to subside. Seven is the perfect distraction.
Sometimes he's like a radio you can turn on and just nod
your head to. He's just dyed his spiky hair a beautiful shade

of dusty rose. He perches on his chair, pushing his cherry red sunglasses up the bridge of his nose, his fingers newly tattooed with tiny blue stars on each. His wallet chain, attached to his baggy, dark blue jeans, jingles when he walks. His new Chucks are hot pink, kicking my legs under the table as he talks excitedly. He's constantly eating but never gains an ounce. His metabolism is the only thing faster than his run-on sentences.

I've decided to fully commit myself to my friendships and not be one of those girls who can't survive without a partner. I am independent, I am going to give all I can to my friends and love them well. They are permanent in a way lovers never can be. Suits me fine. I decide Seven and I will bond in more than a casual roommate and drunken bar-friend way. I ask him details about his life. He shows me photo albums and tells me funny stories. I will seek permanence where permanence really lives — in friendships and family. I go home to Dorval every Monday night for dinner with my parents where we watch sitcoms, and I feel like it calms me.

"How will you erase your short-term memory, hon?" Half-interested.

His mouth moves fast, arms waving in emphatic swirls. "I have a plan, Eve, it's almost too simple."

He shows me a series of lists and graphs I can barely decipher on the paper placemat. I was late to meet him and he created an empire on the thin, rough paper.

"I will accomplish this in four weeks by adopting a strict regime of drugs, sex and debauchery." He goes on to explain that the consumption of illicit things is paramount.

"Yeah, and how is that any different from how you live now?"

"More concentration, more purposeful action!" He doesn't seem to notice my mocking.

He's been letting me sample things lately. Gets a kick out of corrupting me. Last night I tried E for the first time. I threw up. I danced. I don't think I really got it the way you're supposed to.

"More sex, as well, I have to have more sex!"

It's hard to imagine Seven having more sex without giving up things like work, sleep or food. Even right now, the boy at the table by the stairs is looking at Seven in a way you only usually witness on the faces of tigers in nature documentaries.

I, on the other hand, haven't had the requisite rebound love affair. It's been three months of solo sleeps and erotic malaise. Jenny is busy with her boyfriend. Della's friends weren't my friends. Rachel is married to her books and thesis. Melanie takes me out for drinks sometimes. And there are the girls from the women's centre I go to actions with. But I guess if I'm going to concentrate on friends I should try to make some more or connect more intensely with the ones I have. I feel lonely for the first time in my life.

"I'm going to watch a lot of TV, and develop a new sleep pattern." He pushes his finger on the table for emphasis. He shows me a pie chart with 25-minute nap intervals pencilled in red throughout the day. "A guy at the bar works for the cable company. He's stopping by to give us every channel imaginable."

Seven rationalizes that while constantly inundated with images and sound, chemical, sexual and emotional chaos, he will never have to have much thought of the next five minutes, let alone tomorrow.

"I can change the way I feel about time," he says, dipping a key into a tiny baggie of coke he produces from a small heart-shaped pocket he sewed into his soft blue T-shirt, making a half-assed attempt to hide in the shade of the large plastic tree beside our table.

"You should really go to the bathroom to do bumps, honey. We're going to get kicked out again."

Seven doesn't appear to be hearing today. "Eve, I'm trying to tell you that dying will have no meaning."

This from the man who last month barely survived a rooftop jump, eight stories up, wearing only a crash helmet. "I am a T-cell giant!" he'd exclaimed as I dug my nails into my face watching his leap — surrounded by the empty comfort of a gaggle of beer-drinking rooftop friends, stoic in their defence of a fake beach party in the middle of a snowstorm, parkas with hoods pulled up, too drunk to notice the cold. Their mouths suddenly joyfully agape in shock or pride as Seven reached the other side of the alley.

Compared to Jenny, I was a cautious introvert. Compared to Seven, I was a great-grandmother.

I feel myself chew on each cherry as though it were an exercise in precision, pressing the fork tines down on the pastry, turning it all into a pink paste. It's like when you repeat a word too many times, it becomes something else. This cherry between the roof of my mouth and my tongue becomes a ticking clock, its own increment of time.

I take a slow sip of my tea. It's 10:00 a.m. I haven't slept yet. My jaw is slack to one side and I begin to wonder if I look like one of those annoying, greasy raver kids who hang out in the park some mornings, dancing like idiots. I should give up and buy a visor.

Seven leaves a big tip for Chantal, the waitress, whom he has a vague memory of throwing a fork at yesterday. Soon, he will have fully forgotten such small details.

I watch him flitter about the restaurant, stopping to grab the sugar dispenser from the table by the stairs. He holds the jar somewhat suggestively and I'm wondering what happened to his last project, which had involved stapling slices of Wonder Bread to our living-room wall in a checkerboard pattern, taking meticulous care to date each addition with his label maker. "I'm documenting the evolution of mould!" he exclaimed. I wiped day-old liquid eyeliner from my face that had dried while I napped on the sofa.

We've both become big eyed and unambitious in the conventional sense, unlike Rachel, who upon publishing her first small-press book of poetry last month, tattooed her ISBN number across her left tit and took flight. She rides around town in her tapered, red lady wool coat with the classy black buttons on her red tricycle, fearless in the slushy ice, with baskets filled with CVs. Now she's almost finished writing a novel. If we approach her while she sits at the computer in her office she growls like the feral cats in the alley.

She used to take us to her upscale parties filled with industry people, until we began playing scavenger hunts using things we could steal from their homes. She says we have no work ethic and has taken to avoiding us lately, as if our lack of career ambition is contagious. She's been labelling the food in the fridge because we keep getting high and eating her fancy cheese.

When I told Rachel that Della and I broke up, she said, *Finally. There is something off about that girl. I think she's totally full of shit. First of all, what is she, like, 45? And she had that one art show ten years ago that got a lot of press. What has she done since then? She manipulates baby dykes, that's what she does.*

I personally think Rachel could use a little manipulation from someone. She hasn't had a serious girlfriend in a while.

I tried to kiss her once, when we were both on the couch drinking wine and watching *The Breakfast Club*. We could both talk along with the dialogue. I got swept up in the moment. You know the one, where Molly Ringwald takes off one of her diamond earrings and gives it to Judd Nelson and "Don't You (Forget About Me)" features loudly. She laughed, patted my head condescendingly and said, *Sorry, honey, I don't fuck my roommates.*

I hadn't even thought about sex. I just missed kissing. Sometimes, a perfect new-wave soundtrack makes me an illogical romantic.

So while Seven is trying to render time irrelevant, and Rachel tries to fill time with success-making endeavours, I am forever trying to slow it down. I gave up taking buses to the West Island to work at my dad's store. Melanie got me a job at a health-food store in my neighbourhood called Santé! I take naps in the storage room on beds of barley and rice. Melanie and I call it Satan for short.

I light a cigarette, pushing away the plate stained red and gummy. I want time like this with just breath; never frenetic, or too occupied. The arch of my back elastic against the bed frame.

Seven offers me a bump. I decline with a shrug and shake of my head. I can't seem to separate the word "cocaine" from stories with titles like "Eve Has Immediate Heart Attack" or "Eve Turns Into a Junkie Criminal." I was raised on *Degrassi Junior High* and after-school specials. I read all the paperback spinoffs. My Canadian moral core is built on CBC drama plot lines. Seven kisses my cheeks goodbye and leaves me with the cheque. The tiger boy follows him.

Outside on the sidewalk I stand still, feeling every bone in my hands but not my feet. I see three bundles of tulips abandoned on my left and one dead squirrel on my right. It brings tears to my eyes, the little furry guy. I pull a leopard-print hand-kerchief out of my pocket and cover the poor squirrel. I sit on my skateboard at the edge of the curb a few feet down and think about what I should do with my day. Roll to the right. Roll to the left. Pause. Repeat. I know Della is in the park right now with her new dog, or sleeping off a hangover. I make it a practice not to go east of St-Denis for anything. A clean break. I even avoid buying seven-inch records at L'Oblique, my favourite record store. I think about her all the time. I see a white cat across the street jumping up on the dumpster and think of Tomato. I have dreams she comes to me and apologizes for everything and I absolve her. I wake up thirsty. I go to work. I go to class. I go for beer. I wake up and repeat.

Falling asleep briefly with my chin in my hands, I dream about being a guest at Lydia Lunch's sixtieth birthday. Waking up, a truck passes by and exhales exhaust warmth around my ankles. It smells like chocolate.

I feel like I'm having the world's slowest nervous breakdown.

I'm startled out of my dream by Seven, who crouches behind me to squeeze my shoulder, my hair sticking in his lip gloss, his teeth stained red. I see my reflection in his sunglasses, my hair white blond, my face thinner than ever.

"I realized that I never even asked you how you are. I'm so self-absorbed! Are you over her yet? Don't worry if you get sad today. It's just the drugs!" he says, unlocking his low-rider and biking off before I can respond.

When I get home Rachel is sitting on the couch. She's never home during daylight hours. It's jarring. She's wearing a long plaid shirt and grey wool work socks and that's it. She has mascara bruises under her eyes. Her hair is fluffy. On the coffee table in front of her there's an open bag of Ruffles potato chips, a greasy paper bag of warm bagels from Fairmount Bagel and three open containers of cream cheese, salmon paté and what appears to be some sort of onion dip for the chips.

"PMS?" I inquire.

Rachel sighs. I start to wonder if she's had a seizure or a stroke or something. Her eyes are so blank, the pause so pronounced. She reaches under the blanket on the couch and produces a letter.

"Rejection letter from the last publisher."

"For your novel?"

"Yeah."

"Eighteen of the eighteen I sent out."

"What about the publisher who put out your poems?"

"They're about to go under."

Lap covered in chip crumbs, bagel dough stuck between her perfect teeth, she doesn't seem like the confident starlet, the workaholic, precise politico rolling her eyes at her slacker daydreamer roommates. She looks flawed. Her eyes are dark jawbreaker candies, somehow beautiful and anchoring.

I sit next to her on the couch tentatively and reach out for an awkward sideways hug. I'm not sure I've ever touched her before except by accident and that awkward attempt at a kiss rebuffed. Lack of touch defined our roles, as both of us cuddle with Seven constantly, bookend him with platonic affection.

"I smoked all of Seven's pot and got a little hungry." She starts laughing, looking at the empty bags, picking one up to throw across the room, but it doesn't go very far, just lands at the end of the coffee table. I knew at this moment that my friendship with Rachel was circumstantial, that, just like Melanie at the health-food store, we'd be thrown together for a concentrated number of hours and when we moved apart, quit or got fired, we wouldn't really have coffee like we planned to when we ran into each other at the drugstore and scrawled numbers on the backs of our hands. This hug; the time we ran down St-Dominique in the sudden rainstorm on our way to buy toilet paper and smokes, heaving and laughing and soaked through our clothes; the occasional political debate over breakfast. This is what we'll have. And it will be good, solid, limited. In ten years I'll be at a bookstore and I'll see a copy of her novel, a review from *The Globe and Mail* pinned up beside the display of her hardcover accomplishment. I will think about going to the reading, but wonder if she'll remember me. If fame distorts memory. If she'll remember the hug we shared over her rejection letters.

I pull away from her because I realize how bad I smell, and how my jaw aches and how the drugs have worn off completely. I feel like a waste of skin.

"I guess it's back to the women's centre for me." She sighed. Rachel had taken a semester off from coordinating the centre so she could write. She said she was tired of the politics. I watch her get up and go into her room, leaving the mess on the coffee table. I'd never witnessed her not deal with a mess. I picked up the containers and bags, put them away in the kitchen. I could hear Rachel's soft sobs through her thick bedroom door. I almost knock, but decide to leave her be.

I sleep until 3:35 p.m. on the couch. Rachel is pacing in front of me. "Does this look okay?" She's wearing a black cotton dress and some eyeliner, her combat boots.

"You look hot. Where are you going?"

"Seven set me up on a stupid date with some dumb girl I'm probably going to hate."

"Well, that's the right attitude."

She smiled. "I know, I know."

I kiss her on both cheeks and tell her I have to run or I'll be late for my 4:00 p.m. shift. I jump on my skateboard while trying to clear the sleep crust out of my eyes. I start to feel like I have a skeleton again. A man on the street yells, "Why don't you smile, pretty girl? Smile!" I grin and give him the finger.

At the corner of St-Laurent the light is slow to change from red to green. A group of preteens are practicing a Spice Girls dance routine on the sunny sidewalk outside the magazine store on the corner of Duluth. There is a bossy, chubby redhead in high-waisted red pants and Converse high tops trying to tell everyone else what to do. "*Non! C'est pas comme ça!*" And she shows the other girls a jump-up dance move and a kick. I watch her with a huge grin. She has moxy in the bright afternoon sunlight. She turns to look at me, "*Eh? Qu'est-ce que tu veux la?*" I laugh.

"*Rien. C'est cool.*" She stares at me without cracking a smile and turns back to the group to continue the very serious business of spicing up their lives. The other girls look cold and cranky.

11

KICK THEM IN THE KNEES AND THEY'LL GO DOWN FASTER

It's so dead at work that Melanie and I take turns reading and lying on the ground in the storage room while the other minds the cash register. I'm halfway through *Heroine* by Gail Scott. It's changing the way I read. We've developed a system where, if the boss comes in, we cut the CD and cough really loudly. Then whoever is slacking can come out of the storage room with whatever we were restocking diligently. Every once in a while I call Rachel to check on her. She doesn't pick up.

Sitting bent over, arms crossed on a closed white plastic pail of peanut butter, I close the novel and pick at the thumb-holes in the sleeve of my thin black sweater and curl myself into a ball. I notice the silver paint peeling off my boots again and that my socks don't match. I remember suddenly, like a silent musical montage, Della and I the second time we met.

It was the opening for the student vernissage at Dawson College, where I went to CEGEP. I was wearing a short blue dress and platform boots and kept stumbling. I got drunk on the free red wine in plastic cups. Della walked in and straight to me, wearing a leather jacket, dark jeans, button-up white shirt undone over a tank top. Even while people tapped her shoulder and tried to hug her hello, she came up to me like I was the only person in the room and she had a huge secret to tell me. She kissed both my cheeks and smiled, looked right at me. She smelled intoxicating, some sort of men's cologne I'd never smelled before.

I've been thinking about you all day.

If a guy had uttered those words I'd have rolled my eyes, but I couldn't even muster a smirk. Della had called me the night before. She got my number from my teacher and said she'd like to have some wine with me at the opening. I said sure. At least I think so. I was floating above myself the entire two minutes of our phone conversation.

"Good. I'm looking forward to it," she said.

"Me too."

Fearing the lack of anything I could say that would most definitely ruin the perfect phone call I said, *I'm late for work. I'll see you tomorrow night.* I hung up the phone and slid down against the kitchen cupboards, pulling my knees to my chest in a slack-jawed grin. I stared at the chart my mother had recently written on the fridge of things she wasn't going to eat this year, *wheat, dairy, sugar.*

All that day I had spun around like a tornado, re-applying my eyeliner, smoothing down my mini-dress over and over. And then there she stood in front of me, in the middle of the crowded gallery, and put her hands on my waist and held them there. I felt like I was a chess piece in a giant game and she was about to make her move. I was sure she could see my heart coming out of my chest in thrusts like you see in cartoons. I wanted to bury my head in the thick leather collar of her jacket. I was thinking that I might actually die if she didn't kiss me on the mouth right then. The agony of fourteen seconds while she held her lips so close to mine and whispered, *How are you?* I couldn't say anything. I just felt my face go red and hot and my feet dissolving. Finally I couldn't stand it, I grabbed her face with both of my hands and nibbled her bottom lip tentatively before kissing her. The kiss was the best twenty-five seconds I'd had in my life up to that point. When we pulled apart she laughed and said, "I had a feeling that would be ... good."

I was so lost in the memory, feeling that breathless rapture, I didn't hear that Melanie had cut off the Sinead O'Connor CD before letting out a chorus of coughs. The silence seemed appropriate until I saw Marie-Claude's accusatory face peering at me from the storage room door. "Do you have cramps, Eve?"

"Oh, yes, I do." I held my stomach to demonstrate my false pain.

"Well ...?"

"Sorry!"

"*C'est correcte.*" And she smiled. I hate it when bosses act considerate all of a sudden, they should be consistently evil so we don't get sucked into their humanity.

I stand up and straighten my clothes, feel panic that I will soon be fired. I stay twenty minutes late out of guilt and alphabetize the bulk spices.

After work Melanie and I go to a bar on St-Denis for drinks so she can stalk the bartender. The bartender is this little skateboard girl with sandy blond hair and a ball cap and a perpetual old-school Vision Streetwear shirt. She scowls a lot. "She's very arrogant."

Melanie shrugs. "She's also very hot."

She sits there trying to telepathically convince the bartender that she's in love with her. I have three pints and feel warmth spread across my chest. It will do for now, this fake warm happy can keep me going. No one looks attractive to me.

The bartender brings us shots and sits down next to Melanie, letting her know her shift's over. She looks at her like she is definitely her next conquest.

She looks at me across the table briefly, extends her hand. "I'm Nicky."

"I know."

Nicky snorts. Everyone knows who Nicky is. She's the punk rock icon of the lesbian community. I start to wonder if she only owns that one shirt or says much more than a slow heh heh heh pothead laugh.

"You used to go out with Della," Nicky states.

"Yup."

"We used to have a nickname for you."

"Oh yeah, what?"

"Della's Baby Hottie, or D.B.H. Like, 'Hey, there's D.B.H.'"

"Really?" I feel flattered and disturbed at the same time.
"Yeah."

I don't tell Nicky that she once tried to make out with me
in the bathroom at SKY when she was very visibly fucked out
of her tree. I could have been anybody. Della had laughed
about it, said, "Yeah, why don't you go after Nicky?"

"'Cause she's too predictable." Better than admitting how
gross it was that Della was trying to pawn me off on her
buddy.

It is soon very clear that I am becoming the third wheel.
Thankfully, Dave arrives in his red scarf, courier bag overflowing with books. "I saw you through the window," he says.
He joins us for a drink. We talk about East Timor and the
whitewash campaign. We watch Nicky and Melanie engage in
a pre-hook-up ritual, finish two pitchers and head outside.

"Dave, I'm heartbroken."

"Oh. Eve, that sucks. If it's any consolation, so am I."
Dave tells me about the girl he'd been seeing who just left him
for another girl.

"Dave, we need to find you a heterosexual girl."

"I know. But I always end up having crushes on dykes."

"We're good people," I joke.

He smiles at me, and I stop feeling bad for him, he's just
like anyone else with unattainable desires. "You probably fall
for dykes 'cause you're afraid of intimacy."

"No, you're just all hot." Dave must be drunk to say something so un-P.C.

With that I lean in and kiss him, grab him roughly by the
back of the head. We make out against the glass windows

of the bar for a while. A group of guys walk by and start whistling and hollering. I stop mid-grope, feeling empty. I say, "Sorry."

"You don't have to be sorry. That was fun. We should hang out again some time."

"Yeah, call me. We can be broken-hearted together," I say. I begin walking west along Duluth alone, questioning my motives.

I'm heading west along Rachel towards my bike where I'd locked it up outside of work. I feel warm and satiated and independent. Shooting through my veins is the lifeblood of being single and young in this city that shines like vintage jewellery all around me. I think about dating Dave, how easy it would be. He's smart, handsome, looking for love, would never cheat if we were monogamous. Except inevitably I'd become bored. I knew that, even if the idea was appealing. I look up at the cross on the mountain and walk towards it without looking at my feet, playing games with the lights in my head. Completely and entirely content. This city is flawless, this body is so strong right now. I wonder if this is going to be one of those moments I think of when I'm older and my body is frailer and I conjure up moments of strength and adventure, drunken walks home at 2:00 a.m., strutting and smiling.

This is, of course, the perfect moment for a wake-up, I guess. A guy with no belief in gravity or composure crosses the street towards me. You know when you're walking alone and you see someone else, and though they have all the space in the world, you know they are coming right for you anyway? I can see it. The way he crosses the street and looks right at me, nothing could've broken that gaze. I hurry my pace, but don't want to seem scared. I fix a scowl on my lips and grip my keys. I hear Della's voice advising me to look him right in the eye, they are afraid of that. I hear her telling me to always kick them in the knees and they'll go down. If you go for the crotch, you might miss, they might grab your leg. They'll be bigger and faster, just cut them at the knees. God, am I ever paranoid. He probably just wants a light or a cigarette.

"Hey, pretty, hey baby ... where are you going? Can I have your number, where are you going? You want to come with me? You're so pretty, why are you alone tonight? You look like you need a friend, baby, how old are you? You old enough to be out this late?" He is walking beside me now, even though he'd been walking towards me at first.

"First of all, I'm twenty-eight, and I'm married." Plan A. Normally successful.

"No way, you're lying. You're not even eighteen, I bet. You're a baby. You know I'd make a good boyfriend. Why don't you give me a chance?"

He has spit in the corners of his moustache and reeks of whiskey.

"*I'm not interested.*" I look around. Up ahead a man is walking his dog. I speed-walk towards his back. I suddenly feel sober. Every bone is alive and on my side.

"Oh, you're an uptight bitch, aren't you? Aren't you? Yeah, you're a fucking dyke, I bet. You're a fucking lezzie with your big black lezzie boots." He laughs at his own "joke." His breath is becoming laboured walking fast to keep up with me. "What's the matter, you scared of me? I'm not scary. Don't be scared. I just really like you. You're pretty. You could use a boyfriend, I bet."

Plan B. "Fuck off."

I have a pint glass in my coat pocket I stole from the bar. I cup it in my hand. He lunges for my tits and grabs hold of one. I gasp. For a half second it seems like someone has pressed pause.

I pull the pint out and smash it on the sidewalk between us. It crashes. "Get your hands off me asshole!"

Startled, he pauses and takes his hand off my breast and I jog away, towards the man with the dog.

"Hey! Hey! I know I don't know you but that man just grabbed me and I need to pretend we are friends, can I walk beside you?"

"Sure."

"Thanks."

There is an awkward silence.

He looks at me. He could be your regular kind of guy, wearing boring kinds of clothes, like one of the guys I met in school. I look back and the tit-grabber guy is stumbling across the street, still yelling shit at me. I glance back again every few steps and start to feel foolish for getting so scared.

"I don't understand why men are such assholes, you know? I mean, you look like a nice girl. Someone should treat you right. You're so pretty. I mean, I'm a nice guy. Why do girls never go for nice guys? They always leave me for the assholes, you know? I don't know why."

He goes on and on until I picture kicking him in the knees and then in the teeth once he's down. So annoying. He asks for my phone number and I say that I'm married, hiding my left hand in my coat pocket.

"I'd never let my wife out this late at night by herself. Take my number, take my card, c'mon, just take it. You won't regret it. I think we were meant to meet tonight. I'm sure of it. I'm so sure. It's fate."

He talks about this myth he's created in the last five minutes as though it were the gospel. But by then I am on the Main and I grab the grey paper cardboard rectangle, defeated, say, "Hey thanks, gotta go." I leave him in mid-sentence. I hear him yell, "Fine! Fuck! I have the *worst* luck! Fucking women!" I get to where my bike is locked outside of work, unlock it and push each foot down frantically, passing the drunks outside the CopaCabana, the hippies outside the veggie co-op café, ending up at home in less than three minutes. Locking up my bike I notice the fullness of the moon, the reason everyone seemed extra-unhinged tonight. Shaking, mood ruined and totally sober.

Rachel isn't home. The apartment is really quiet, empty. The kitchen is in the back of the apartment with windows overlooking the courtyard below and a balcony messy with bottles and abandoned plants. I check every seam between inside and out. I turn on all the lights, I open and close each kitchen cupboard. I turn on the stereo, turn up the soothing sounds of Tiger Trap. I pull on a nightgown and relax into its ugly comfort. I check all the locks on both doors and look closely at each window in my bedroom that overlooks the street, wondering if they could be pushed open. I walk from room to room monitoring each strange sound.

The phone rings four times. There is no one on the other end. Just static. I unplug the phones. I can't deal.

I watch the *X-Files* and read an article in a magazine about how to get out of a trunk if you're being kidnapped. Apparently, you just kick out the tail lights and wriggle your fingers, try to catch the attention of cars behind you. A woman in Baltimore saved herself this way, because a passing car called the police when they saw her hands popping out of the trunk. I fall asleep and dream about aliens and confined spaces. I wake up feeling very uneasy when Seven stumbles in at 3:00 a.m. yelling that he's going to make the best raspberry crepes I have ever tasted in my life and drags my limp body into the kitchen, brightly lit by every available light.

"Rachel's not home. Isn't that weird?" I can't shake this creeped-out feeling.

Seven says, "Yes! Oh, that's awesome!" He measures out flour in the Pyrex measuring cup.

He explains, "She was going on a date tonight. Finally! I set her up with Amanda from the hospice. She's butch ..." Seven holds one finger out, "she's working-class," he taps a second finger, "and ..." he makes a fake drum roll on his knees, "she reads! Jackpot!" Seven volunteers as a peer counsellor at an AIDS hospice, a place he told Rachel and me was a hotbed of politically conscious lesbian activity.

"Oh, yeah, she was trying on outfits this afternoon. I forgot."

After insisting that indeed Seven's raspberry crepes were the best ever, good enough to open a restaurant that only serves said crepes, and only to the most worthy customers, we fall into the couch starch-heavy and warm. We spoon together and he runs his fingers through my hair. "Eve, I really like you. I think you're solid."

My heart bursts. I say, "Thanks, Seven, you rock my world."

When Seven gets up to put our well-worn VHS copy of *Hairspray* into the VCR, he turns to me and pauses. I worry that something is stuck to my face or that I'm suddenly bleeding from my eyes and I don't realize it.

"What?"

"I'm kind of glad you had this break from Della. I mean, she's cool and everything and I love her guts but ... she's not the most honest person in the world."

"Well, obviously."

"No, I mean, beyond the cheating. I think there's a lot we don't know about her. It's just a hunch."

"Rachel says that too, that she thinks she's full of shit."

"I hope she's not a narc," he smirks, lighting his little glass bong.

"Definitely not disciplined enough to be a cop."

We go to bed after watching *Hairspray* for what must be the eleventh time.

We wake up to a persistent doorbell and banging on the door. *Della!*

I stumble down, half-hoping, half-cringing. I practise looking cold and annoyed.

But standing on the front steps are two cops. I'm so surprised I actually gasp. They look like actors. I don't think I've ever gasped that audibly before. I yell up the stairs to "Seven, um, it's the pi — the, uh, cops!" I hear Seven running into his room, presumably to hide some things. I wonder quickly if I could actually lie convincingly to the police that Seven is my boyfriend. I practise looking completely innocent, doe-eyed, eight years old under the weight of their stares. They take off their hats. They say they've been trying to call, I remember how I unplugged the phones.

After they speak a few words, I run up to get him, they follow me, heavy boots landing on the downbeat of a song in my head.

"Seven, you should hear this, you won't fucking believe this."

I open his door. "Seven! They're not here for you." I whisper harshly. "Something happened to Rachel."

Seven comes out from under the bed, walks out of his bedroom pretending he was just sleeping. "What's going on?"

The police said the kinds of things police say when fucked-up shit happens to pretty young women. Their billy clubs shone in the light of our door.

When someone tells you something that is completely unbelievable, too horrible to not be a fiction, too much like TV or like a nightmare you've had, it makes you feel so bizarre. When the cops said, "Sorry, madame, your roommate, she had your address in her wallet. Stephen was her emergency contact number, we tried to call. There is no easy way to say this."

12

MONTREAL *GAZETTE*

MARCH 1996

HATE SLAYING OF LESBIAN WOMAN STUNS MONTREAL: TWO NEO-NAZI SKINHEADS CHARGED.

Rachel Brown, a twenty-six-year-old graduate student at McGill University was attacked by two men on St-Dominique Street south of Ontario on Tuesday just after midnight. She was pronounced dead on arrival at St. Luc's Hospital.

John Webster, twenty-four, of Kirkland, and Gaetan Faucher, nineteen, of Lachine, both neo-Nazi skinheads known to police, were arrested attempting to flee the scene. A neighbour called 911 when she heard shouting and commotion on the street below. There are believed to be more suspects at large.

Witnesses say Brown had been kissing another woman outside the Metropolis nightclub. The other woman, who asked not to be identified, went back into the club. Brown began to walk home where it is believed she was followed and targeted for being gay.

"This is a clear case of gay bashing," says Charlene Mayor, spokesperson for the Lesbian and Gay Student group at McGill, where Brown was an active member.

There will be a candlelight vigil on the corner of St-Dominique and Ontario at 8:00 p.m. on Wednesday, March 20.

13

—⁓—

EVERYBODY IS HIV+

On the day of the funeral, I don't know what comes over me. I pick up the cordless and press seven digits. Della's number is memorized like dance steps in my fingers, though I could no longer recite them properly if asked. It rings twice. I hang up. The apartment is so cold, the kind that makes you want to take seven baths even though your skin is rubbed raw. I've been living in the claw-foot tub, surrounded by candles and staring at the framed print of a painting by Toulouse-Lautrec on the ivory wall. By the time I get out of the scorching water it has turned tepid, skin slick with lavender oil; I stand in the kitchen dripping careless rivers onto the black and white tile, reading Seven's note with directions to the church. He's gone to meet Rachel's family.

Slipping my legs into the hollow of my borrowed dress and pulling the straps over red-dry shoulders I realize I can't zip it up properly. I can't reach around. Melanie had shown up with it last night, placed lightly on top of a bag filled with Tupperware bowls of veggie stews, chilies and cupcakes. "I'm rural. When you're sad, I have to feed you," she explains. Everything I own is ripped, splattered in paint, low-cut, light distances above the knee — so she lent me her respectable job-interview dress for the funeral. We sat in my living room, drinking wine, and I felt the weight of the empty apartment. Rachel's parents had left after hours of sorting through her things.

"Can I do anything for you, Eve? Anything at all."

"No, that's okay." Stay. Just stay the night. Don't leave me alone.

"Are you sure, sweetie? 'Cause I can just call Nicky and cancel."

"No, no, I'm totally fine." See that I'm lying. Please notice.

Melanie got up and hugged me, I detected some relief in her posture as I watched her walk down the stairs. I hoped Seven would come home. He didn't. I remembered he was going to see the Run DMC reunion show up the street. I took an Ivan and went to bed shivering. My mother called and offered to come pick me up. I said I was fine. She didn't push it.

Groggy with a Valium headache, standing half naked in my room, freezing and flush with red from the hot bath, I am overwhelmed with the need for someone familiar. I call her again. After I hang up, I can't even remember what I said, or be sure that I actually made the call until Della shows up within fifteen minutes.

Standing in my room, helping me zip up my dress, she doesn't talk about herself for even one moment. It's like *Invasion of the Body Snatchers* — her beautiful angular boyish frame, her hair a little longer, less blue and more reddish-brown like her childhood photos. Same black hoodie hanging on her shoulders laissez-faire, this time over a tucked-in dress shirt and some black tuxedo pants with a stripe of shine down the seams, she calls them her funeral-wedding pants. The same Converse sneakers. She hugs me harder than she ever has. Zips up my dress with no questions.

"You're going to be okay."

"I'm not. I'm really not." I feel myself falling. I sit down on the couch and stare off slack-jawed. She crouches on the coffee table in front of me.

"You will. Seven will, too, in time."

"Seven's been to a hundred funerals but I don't know how he's going to handle this one. There was no way to prepare. It wasn't her time. It was fate. She wasn't sick, she wasn't an old soul who lived a full fucking life! She was robbed, Della, fucking robbed!"

"Yes, she was."

"I dream every night about killing those skinheads. I picture it, I picture stabbing them until they're dead. I picture hurting their fathers, whoever made them who they are, just blood everywhere." Della holds me on the couch while I cry. The phone rings and rings and I don't pick it up. She reminds me of the time and we stand up, I wash my face hurriedly in the bathroom sink. I look older.

She walks me outside and hails a cab. It's March but it may as well be February, we are bundled in layers of coats and scarves, my stockings have runs almost immediately. All seams bursting. When she tries to apologize for cheating I push my hand to her mouth. "No rules this time. None. Deal?"

"Deal."

In the days between Rachel's death and funeral, I've been trying to hold Seven together, unsuccessfully. We stayed up for the rest of that night, making calls and arrangements. We just kept going. I wasn't sure what my role should be, after all, I was the roommate. I couldn't say exactly how well I knew Rachel, but I was there, with her things, with her best friend in the world. I took over the practical details that take over a death, and helped as best I could. After they were dealt with, we sat on the couch for a whole day.

We cuddled up. Seven felt like a moth. No bones, just string. Every once in a while he'd tell me a story about Rachel, from when she was younger. When they were obsessed with the Encyclopedia Brown books and formed their own detective agency. Rachel would give her old dresses and dolls to Seven to play with in the tree fort they built in the back woods. They kept a padlock around a box Rachel's grandmother had given her as a hope chest. Before they even knew anything about sex, they knew they were different, before there was the language to explain it, there was just this feeling that brought them together.

After drinking a pot of coffee, we decided to go get a tattoo. Simple, typewriter font, Rachel's favourite font, the year of her birth and death. We didn't talk on the way there, or on the way back.

Rachel's parents decided to have a funeral in Montreal, at the chapel at McGill's, before having one in her hometown. She didn't know anyone back home anymore anyway.

The chapel is packed to overflowing. Seven looks frail and childlike in his black suit; he sits with Rachel's parents whom he's known since he was a child. They look shell-shocked.

I kick my feet under the pew and keep crying until I can't anymore. I pick lint off of my dress. There is a rift between family and friends in the church, a weirdness that comes when your closest family has no idea who your closest friends are. Two camps that loved the same person separately, like there were two funerals happening at once.

Rachel's parents are quiet, her mother sheds some tears during Seven's eulogy, while her father is stoic. I keep hearing what they'd said when they came to gather her things two nights before the funeral. "I always knew nothing good could come from this lonely lifestyle. If she'd only made different choices."

"What about the skinheads? What if they'd made different choices? What if you'd chosen to love your daughter instead of ignoring her for years?"

I wasn't able to stop myself. Seven had dragged me out onto the balcony, but still we could hear her mother's sobs. I felt awful, ashamed, but also angry.

"C'mon Seven, can you picture Rachel lonely? She was always complaining she didn't get enough time alone to work on her writing. Everyone wanted to be around her. She didn't date much because everyone wanted her and she was picky. I hate thinking that her parents picture her as this lonely freak."

"I'll try to talk to them, Eve. I've known them since I was

a baby. I'll try. They're just hurting right now. We need to respect that."

Seven went back inside, and helped pack up her belongings, the ones her mother wanted to keep. He arranged for women from the Concordia Women's Centre to come over the next night to sort through her books and papers, give them to the archives, the library at the women's centre.

I went back into my room, a mix of guilt and anger. I put on a red dress and electric blue eyeshadow and went to the Miami bar for drinks. I left quietly without saying goodbye to Seven or Rachel's parents. On the street the sidewalk felt uneven and eyes felt like tiny snow globes. It was hard to swallow.

The bartender looked so much like Rachel — black boots, tough smile, choppy black and red hair — I felt like I might throw up. I couldn't open my mouth to say anything. "Hey," she said, "you were Rachel's roommate."

"Yes, I was." I looked at her questioningly.

"I sat on a jury with her at McGill. She used to come drink here a lot after meetings. I still can't believe it." She wiped down the bar with her white cloth.

"I know."

"What'll it be?"

"Uh, a pint of red."

"Okay." She turned her back and I closed my eyes tight. I drank the beer at a table by the window and bit my lip until it bled. I missed Della so much I felt dizzy. I went back home a little squirrelly, called Melanie from the pay phone to ask to borrow a dress for the funeral. Bought a bottle of wine on the way home from the corner store.

The night after Rachel was murdered my mother stopped by with some muffins and a box of groceries, worried about how we were holding up. She filled the fridge with orange juice, spinach, eggs. The freezer with pre-packaged waffles, micro-wavable fettuccine in boxes, veggie pizzas, suburban food. She did the dishes, mopped the floor, rubbed Seven's shoulders. She took six bottles of St. Ambroise beer out of the cardboard case and arranged them on the fridge door, taking out the old crusty ketchup bottles and pouring all the soy sauces into one bottle. Seven and I sat in the kitchen butter-ing the slabs of cranberry nut bread and chewing solemnly. It was the first time my mother had come over and stayed longer than five minutes since I moved in. Seven got up in the mid-dle of our stilted conversation to smoke on the balcony and drink one of the beers she brought over.

"Mom, it's important to me that if something were to happen to me, you'd know it wasn't because I was gay, it would be because someone was homophobic. You know that right? I mean ..." I should probably have backed up a bit, but the grief was confusing me. "You know I'm gay, right?"

She paled. "Well, I'm not stupid. I've noticed certain things changing in your life." She continued to scrub at a stubborn stain on the kitchen table, likely collage glue from one of my art projects.

"Yeah, well, I realized when Rachel's parents came over that I couldn't live that way, with my family hating me for being who I was. So I just thought I'd stop being chicken and tell you, and make sure ... you know, you'd be supportive."

"Well, first of all, I doubt her parents hated Rachel. You wouldn't know because you're not a parent yet, but it's just not possible." For the first time my mother was being impossibly naive. "Your father and I are very liberal people, Eve. You know that. We believe in tolerance. We didn't want to raise you the way we were raised, you know, to be scared of everything."

I felt a little angry man rising in my throat, like a cartoon character. It almost makes me giggle. I sipped my beer slowly. I don't want to be tolerated, I want to be accepted.

"Rachel's parents actually told her she was going to burn in hell. Her father once told her she wasn't welcome in their home for an entire year. They'd finally got to the point where she could come home for Christmas and they would be nice to her, but she couldn't mention anything about being gay. They never met her partners. They never really knew her."

"Well, they're from a different generation. It's different. Your grandmother didn't approve of me because I wore pants, most of my relatives don't talk to me because I won't submit to my husband and I wanted to finish high school."

I have no idea how to speak to that. I didn't want to get into another story of how the Mennos almost ruined her life path.

"Anyway, I'm going to go clean your bathroom. It's disgusting."

She left shortly after, asking me to move home again and handing me forty bucks. I hugged her goodbye extra long. I watched her pull away from the window seat. I called her to leave a thank-you message on her machine, to promise to come home on the weekend for dinner.

After the funeral, Della, Seven and I took the 24 bus back across the city. We walked up St-Urbain, stopping to buy booze and spray paint, manically talking about everyone at the funeral.

The rest of the night is blurred. I woke up with my head against a table at the Main, a blurry vision of Seven and Della eating smoked meat sandwiches and laughing and crying, a mix of the two.

We have been getting a lot of calls, from people who didn't even really know Rachel all that well. At the vigil the day before the funeral, I felt so strange and outside myself. We held candles, there were impassioned speeches from Rachel's close friends. Every time I saw a dyke I heard them talking about *The girl who got bashed. There's the girl whose room-mate got bashed.* People I barely knew tried to hug me. Friends of mine were awkward. Rachel had become a celebrity almost, and anyone attached to her was afflicted with this status. It felt almost like people wanted to have known her, or relayed stories like, *Oh, I saw her read a poem once at the café, it was really good.* Then they'd pause and look really sad. Or, *One time we had a class together and she liked my paper. She was really smart.* And a tear would run down their faces.

Amanda, the girl who had been on a date with Rachel that night, hasn't been to work since it happened. Seven has been dropping by her apartment, but she doesn't answer. Her roommate says she went to her parents' house to deal with her shock. How could your life not unravel into the same scene replaying, choosing to go back into the bar rather than walk her home. It would have ruined me. I can't imagine. I don't. I try not to.

Everyone is also very fearful about being next. Dyke Defence organizers taught more classes, the women's centre at Concordia made stickers of weak points on the male body, journalists wanted quotes for their newspapers. News reporters interviewed the neighbours of the two suspects. *They were such nice boys. They mowed my lawn every summer.* They all looked so shocked, but I recognized those men as two of dozens I had to contend with in high school, avoid while waiting for the bus at Dorval circle. They were fuelled by indignant rage, those boots and laces games I knew before I turned twelve, the colour coding, not looking into their eyes because I knew they were dead inside and I couldn't risk catching what they had. Running through my head — what I would do if I had to step in and defend a person of colour or a gay guy they'd decided to attack. What if it were just me there, and I had to risk my life? Would I? It was only after I'd started dating Della that I realized I was no longer someone who could hide in my privileged skin at the bus stop when the skinheads passed by, who could afford to spit at their boots and give them nasty looks. Kissing Della goodbye at the Metro now made me a target as well. It also made me realize how normal it had been growing up to see them, like it was no big deal at all.

There was this collective grief that took over the queer community after Rachel's death. It made me bond to anyone who looked queer on the street, or anyone I knew from the bars, or actions. It gave us all the permission to look each other in the eye, to smile or nod, to acknowledge each other's presence and it felt oddly like we were forming this army together, silently, without anyone really ever leading us. Instead of feeling scared, I got bold. I made out with girls on the streets, I held Melanie's hand just to be visible. I wore Queer Nation and ACT UP T-shirts I'd borrowed from Della months before, I scrawled Everybody is HIV+ across T-shirts my mother had ordered me from the Sears catalogue. I tasted pepper on my tongue before I got raging headaches and thought of Rachel every day. I stopped going home to visit my family, not able to handle the suburbs, risk seeing skinheads while on my way to the corner store to buy my mother milk. Something was bubbling under my skin and I couldn't understand it. It was rage.

The women's centre becomes a home base for anti-violence action. Someone suggests re-naming the centre after Rachel, another person starts a mural. A 'zine of poetry is edited. I watch it all happen with a detached sense of wonder and relief, empowered but exhausted. I don't go to class. I sleep on the women's centre couch.

At home Seven, Della and I have started bunking up at night, curling around each other in sleep, or fake sleep. All I could do was run through Rachel's last days like a movie, remember words I said to her, try to picture her face. I couldn't really see her clearly. I woke up in the middle of the night crying. My dreams were tears. The wetness against my pillow startled me awake. The air in my bedroom was hard and chalky.

Della becomes the den mother, watering the plants, taking care of Gertrude Stein, who has taken to sleeping on our backs.

She doesn't go home at all, ever. I hear her on the phone some-times, asking someone to take care of Tomato. I don't ask who. When Seven and I are at work, she takes our sheets to the laundromat and washes all the towels that have become hard, stinking paper plates of neglect. When I come home the coffee table in our angular living room is cleared of chip bags, empty cigarette packs, ninety-nine-cent pizza-slice crusts. A vase of flowers sits like a bull's eye on the green table. We come home to an organized fridge, a shower stall free of mildew. I don't know where Della is getting her money and making her way in the world, and I don't ask. She and I move into the space of being intimate strangers, we see each other every day, but there are certain things we don't talk about any more. Money. xxxx. Our breakup. We are now truly inde-pendent, but deciding to hang out a lot. It makes a difference knowing this. If she were to leave, I'd be surprised, but not devastated.

14

———∽∽∽———

MY BODY IS A BATTLEFIELD
AND IT WANTS
CRACKER JACKS

Lately my insomnia gets so pronounced it's like another being sitting in the room with me. Sometimes it's infectious, and Della, Seven and I move furniture around, glue Scrabble letters to the walls, make 'zines and draw comics. At 2:00 this morning, Seven brings out a scrapbook, overflowing, one of those photo albums with clear adhesive pages. He opens it across his lap, sitting up in my bed, lights a joint and passes it around. The album contains page after page of obituaries, fading photographs of friends smiling in black and white with dates underneath, inspirational prayers. So many pages of so many young men it takes my breath away. He points at each reflection, tells a story about how he knew each of them.

"This was my first lover, this was my drama teacher, this was the trick who paid my tuition at McGill, I was in a punk band with this guy when I was 18, this," he pauses, "was Rachel's uncle, the first gay guy I ever met. She was the only one in her family to go to his funeral." I don't know what to say. Seven seems so casual pointing everyone out to me, like it's a yearbook. There are newspaper clippings from rallies and protests. Della nods, I note that she is not fazed.

"How is this even possible? That so many people you've known and loved are dead?" I move my slow molasses tongue around in my sticky mouth, close my reddened eyes in a slow blink.

Della and Seven look blankly at me, the way they do sometimes. They exchange a look of mutual disbelief. "Oh Eve," Della says. It sounds almost like an accusation. I point to a date on the newspaper clipping. "I was eleven!" But I know what they mean.

"It's different now, guys are living longer, with the cocktails and everything," Seven says. "I think you're really lucky."

Della doesn't look so gracious. Her face looks blank.

He puts the scrapbook down, pointing to a clipped photo from the Montreal *Mirror*. "Shit, Della, that's you and I at the protest after Sex Garage! I didn't know you were there too!" Della is holding a placard that says, *We're here, we're queer, get used to it!*

They start to tell each other what they remember about that night and the nights that followed.

"Eve, you'd never believe what happened that summer. People went fucking nuts. Everyone was like, oh, you don't want us to be queer? You're going to beat us up for being queer? We'll show you queer!"

"Yeah, girls were just fucking everywhere! And fags would check their pants at the coat check and were just blowing each other right out in the open at the bar. It was unreal."

Seven gets out of bed, putting the rest of a joint out in the stand-up ashtray beside my bed, exhaling. "I want Cracker Jacks. I'm going to go find them."

"Be careful," I say. I turn to Della and kiss her hard, dissolve into her embrace. Afterwards we lie spooning, naked crescent moons.

"Hey Della. Have you ever been tested?"

"No, I never shot any dope, only fucked two guys in high school, both virgins."

"Oh."

"You?"

"Once in grade ten. The free clinic insisted. Negative. The last time I went the counsellor said the rate of transmission for lesbian sex was so low it didn't make sense to test me."

"Seven's positive right?"

"I never asked. I assume so, just by things he says, you know, infers, the way he alludes to it."

"Gerard told me he definitely is ... I just wondered if you knew."

"I thought you're not really supposed to talk about someone else's status like that."

"Ideally."

"It's weird how he doesn't, like, take lots of vitamins and he drinks and does so many drugs, like he doesn't care."

"Well, you have to keep living and having fun, right?"

"I suppose. I think I might try to up my chances."

"You want to be like those ladies who shop at Santé!?"

"Never!" I picture the parade of pale, lifeless hypochondriacs who stock up weekly on whatever the newest cure for everything is, shark fins, wheatgrass, whatever. But they never look happy or well, no matter how much they fork over.

"I wish you could only get AIDS from giving money to Jerry Falwell," mumbles Della. "I read that somewhere and I totally agree." Her eyes close involuntarily and she snaps into a deep snore. I sit in the window seat watching the shadows in the park, waiting for two hours until Seven comes home. I jump into bed before he comes in, in case he wants to join us. Walking out into the living room I see a new pair of shoes at the door and realize he is not alone.

I fall asleep happy we are all safe in the house, for now. It's the only time of day I stop panicking.

The phone rings. I don't answer it. It rings again. "Allo?"

Silence. Breath.

I hang up and my heart goes crazy, certain, absolutely, that it was Rachel trying to talk to us from beyond. I wake up Della and show her the number I wrote down from the call display. Her face is blank. She calls the number. No one picks up.

"What? Who is it?"

"Nothing. No one."

"No, you know who it was."

Silence.

"Whose number is it?"

She buries her head under the covers mumbling xxxx's name.

Oh. I feel somewhat relieved that it's not Rachel's ghost, though the thought was somewhat comforting depending on how you looked at it.

I poke Della's back, whisper, "Are you guys talking a lot lately?"

"No. I don't know why she'd call this late. I don't even know how she'd get this number."

"Seven's listed."

"Oh."

"It's 3:00 a.m., maybe something's wrong. Maybe you should call her back."

Della lifts the covers off dramatically. "Eve, c'mon. You'd really be okay with that?"

"No rules, remember? If she's your friend, you might want to check in with her?" Stop the burning, I tell myself. Be an adult.

"Nah, she's fine. She's got Isabelle."

"They got back together?"

"They never broke up."

"Oh." Suddenly I felt like a horrible dramatic person who overreacted. Then it switched to anger and betrayal. Then to wondering if Della was telling me the truth. Something in my gut said she wasn't.

"Does Isabelle know that you guys slept together?"

"I don't know. I never asked."

As if they never discussed it. This was thoroughly unsatisfying. But in the grand scheme of things, which is the only way I'd been able to think of things since Rachel's death, monogamy didn't matter. If I had any inclination to, I could do whatever I wanted. It seemed that just now Della and I didn't feel like acting on anything outside of us, however undefined.

I wake up in the morning, Della still dreaming, Seven asleep on the couch and his guest's shoes gone. I make a pot of coffee and do the dishes, stopping only a few times to cry, and the tears come like sighs or sneezes, moments of wonder, and pass just as quickly. I watch little chubby birds on the railing of the balcony off the kitchen. The morning light is soft and perfect. Montreal seems at peace. Slipping on my sneakers, toque and hoodie over my sleepy shirt and PJ bottoms, I scuffle down the stairs counting change in my open palm, enough to get cream at the dep. As I reach the middle of the stairway I am jolted from my peaceful solitude by the doorbell. Persistent. It reminds me of the night Rachel died and the sound makes me want to throw up.

I open the door expecting Jehovah's Witnesses but instead it's my parents. My mom in a red fleece jacket with an over-compensating-for-my-dead-friend smile, my dad in his sturdy leather motorcycle jacket, both holding out empty wicker baskets. My dad has combed his greying curly red hair from receding hairline down into a slight ponytail, one Seven has taken to calling the "oldmanytail." He wears his favourite faded Rolling Stones tour shirt.

"Wow, hi. You surprised me!" I rub my eyes hoping to smudge last night's makeup away.

"We're driving to the country to pick apples and you're coming with us!"

"What? Why didn't you call? It's so early. I don't understand."

"We tried Eve. We left four messages last night." Oh, yeah, I'd skipped them all in anticipation of a message from Rachel's ghost or xxxx.

"Oh, oh, okay. Come on in. You closed the store?"

"Nope, Alex is taking over for the day. It's quiet these days." They follow me up, I motion towards the couch and put my finger against my lips in a shh.

I do not want to go, I feel confused and still dreaming.

"When we get home, we'll make pies, freeze them and then eat them for Thanksgiving," my mom whispers, straightening a photo frame in the hallway where they wait for me to get dressed.

Thanksgiving was in a few weeks. How did it get so late in the season? Thanksgiving was always a fairly fun day at our household, but this year everything looked different. I wasn't finding comfort in pies and place settings, familiar after-lunch walks, conversations about cousins' weddings. I'd been dreading the impending dinner.

I pull on some jeans and a sweater, kiss sleeping Della and Seven goodbye. When I get to their car, I see there's a bed frame tied to the car roof and Jenny in the backseat. "Surprise! We brought Jenny."

I haven't seen Jenny in months. She smiles at me, in sunglasses, holding an oversized takeout cup of coffee. I wonder how they convinced her to come along. I felt suddenly awkward, even though I was sitting in a car with three people I'd known my whole life, who knew me the best, but it didn't feel that way anymore. They felt like strangers, the quantity of time they spent with me versus the quality of time with my newest friends.

The car ride towards Ste-Anne-de-Bellevue was awkward and quiet, the occasional burst of small talk. The topics Jenny and I could broach with my parents were limited.

"Jenny told us she can give you her old bedroom set so you can finally move up off that futon on the ground. That's why it's tied to the roof. Isn't that great?"

My mom leans back from the front seat, pausing briefly from berating my father for driving too fast or too slow. She asks about school, student loan applications, about working at the health-food store. My dad tells me about a new guitar he got in the store, asks again when I'll come pick up some shifts. I say *soon*, he says *great* and we both know this isn't the case.

At a roadside washroom Jenny, fixing herself in the mirror while I pee, says, "I told a regular at work that I really wanted a new bed frame, one of the metal ones from IKEA, and he had one delivered to the club. Can you believe it? Anyway, my mom bought me that wood one last year, so you can have it. I mentioned it to your mom, because when she picked me up it was just sitting in our hallway ready for Goodwill. Thought they could drive it over for you later."

"Yeah, sounds good."

I exit the stall, straighten my skirt. "He just delivered it to the bar?"

"Yeah. Strange eh? One time a guy brought me a rice cooker, 'cause I'd mentioned I wanted one, but a bed frame, that's a real coup. All the other girls were jealous."

She hands me her tube of chapstick. It smells like butterscotch mints. I run it over my lips. I look pale.

"I'm sorry about Rachel, Eve. I didn't even know until I read about it in the paper, and then I felt weird calling you and stuff."

"That's okay. It's been crazy at the apartment, trying to keep Seven's spirits up."

"Yeah, I bet."

"And Della and I, we're sort of back on again."

"Really? But she cheated."

"I know, I know." I shrug. For some reason I couldn't relay the complexities involved to Jenny in a truck stop bathroom on a three-minute break from the pleasant silence with my parents.

"How is work, anyway?"

Jenny shrugged. "It's a job. I took some shifts at a massage parlour, too."

"I wrote a pro-sex-work paper for my women's studies class this semester about how sex work and feminism are not mutually exclusive."

"Oh yeah?" Jenny made a face.

"What?"

"Well, let me tell you. Stripping is not feminist. Everyone will rip you off if they can, other girls, men, everyone. It's like going back in time to when feminism didn't exist, except you can make good money sometimes. I read that book you lent me about that girl in San Francisco at the peep show and I hated it. I threw it against the wall. It's not therapeutic. It's hard work. It's boring."

I didn't know what to say.

"But touch my thigh," she said, putting my hand on her right leg. "Rock hard, baby! Plus, these boots cost $300." She smiled.

At the apple orchard, Jenny climbs to the top of one of the trees, even in her heeled boots. My mom takes a photo of her hanging upside down, while I stand on the ground beside her. We fill plastic bags with tart, perfect fruit.

On the ride home Jenny tells my parents all about Jack, her boyfriend, the jock. They are more interested than I've ever heard them be about almost anything. By the time we drive back into Montreal, they knew more about the jock who once called me *that weird lesbian witch girl* than Della, Seven or anyone else in my life I'd put down as an emergency contact number. I stop listening. I watch the fields turn into subdivisions, into factories, Montreal West, NDG, winding up the hill by the hospitals, into the plateau.

My mom and dad both hug me close to say goodbye. They feel warm and safe in one moment and like complete strangers the next. I was itching to be back at the apartment with Della and Seven.

With two plastic bags of apples in my arms, I helped my dad struggle with the wooden headboard of Jenny's old bed frame up the stairs.

Della and Seven are curled up on the couch watching an afternoon TV movie, *Footloose*, like siblings. My dad nods polite hellos in their direction, as though they were amicable strangers on a street corner.

My dad helps put together the wooden bed frame while my mother drives Jenny home. I showed him some artwork from school, some paintings inspired by Rachel's poems. I feel embarrassed of them all of a sudden, and put them away quickly.

He gives me an extra-long goodbye hug. He smells like smoke and woodsy soap and coziness.

I sink between Seven and Della on the couch and watch a young Sarah Jessica Parker dance her heart out. I cry heavy sobs while Kevin Bacon kicks out the jams. Della and Seven are silent. Sobbing had become so commonplace, it no longer startles.

We smoke a joint and I fall asleep, waking to the smell of apple pies from an industrious Della. She and Seven are singing Dolly Parton's greatest hits.

The apartment smells like home.

I walk into the kitchen, accepting a plate of warm apples and pastry. "Della, you should move in."

Seven looked up from his plate. "Yeah, sure. You totally should."

Della leaves a few hours later, returning with Tomato in a cat carrier and a duffle bag of important objects. We decide she will sleep in my room, store her things in Rachel's old room, a door we haven't opened since the funeral.

Seven sits at the kitchen table with the typewriter and a stack of papers. "I'm writing a play."

"That's so gay."

"It would be gayer to write an AIDS memoir." He laughs, before jumping back to the keys pounding out words.

In the bathroom medicine cabinet I notice an empire of pill bottles. New ones. I ask Seven about it.

"Well," he says, opening the balcony door and selecting a cigarette from his pack, "I'm not a sudden fan of western medicine or the pharmaceutical companies, but I don't know. I'm not ready to go."

"I'm not ready for you to go."

He smiles, opens the door. Della walks up behind me, putting her muscled arms around my torso.

15

———✦✦✦———

LITTLE SPLEENS
OF TRUTH

December is like cutting your tongue. The strongest muscle month, clenched, expecting impact on frozen sidewalks. The air smells like the sharp reality of what's to come. Beads of cold blood and soft skin imprinted with the wrist of my too-tight winter jacket worn begrudgingly. I buy an ice blue bra with pink roses and lace trim. Matching panties. Try to cheer myself up. The roses poke through my T-shirt and make my chest look lumpy. I take it off. I've been dreaming about Holly Hobbie, my favourite bedsheets as a kid. I had a vision or a premonition last night of a woman in a fur coat. It wasn't a good vision. I was almost asleep. It could have been nothing. But it felt like something.

The problem with true stories is they always end in loss. Sometimes the difference between fiction and non is almost arbitrary. They both ask: *who are we?* Sometimes I can't tell where Della telling the truth begins and Della telling the truth ends. I get these instinctual punches in the gut.

Lately she's too depressed to lie, or instill suspicion. Della doesn't do anything. She is fading into the fabric of her trademark black hoodie. It's beginning to feel like I have a human pet instead of a girlfriend. I'm questioning my urge to fill that role in my life. I try to think of myself as my own girlfriend. Her ability to speak breaks down into guttural mumbles and pre-verbal sounds. That I'm in love with her is a memory, a postcard on the fridge. I almost wish she'd go flirt with other girls just so I can wash the sheets, and see a glimpse of that girl from the art opening at school.

Once she said to me that her biggest fear was that she'd never succeed at anything. Just a legacy of unfinished plans, half-stitched projects, broken-hearted bitter girls in her wake. It's a few weeks before her thirtieth birthday when she's supposedly going to kick it. She seems to be trying to stop her heart with boredom. What would I do if all my life, my family said I'd die before I was thirty, like my mother, grandmother and aunts?

Our conversation this morning:

"I don't mean to pry, but you are making everything worse by sleeping all the time. You need to get up."

Silence.

Eventually she says, "Hmhmhmm I don't wannuh."

We've had the same ephemeral back and forth every

morning for three weeks. She is living up to her own expectation of ruin and she smells like hopelessness. Her skin used to intoxicate me, her face would bring to mind warm vanilla and almond tea. Now she emanates this eggshell tang, a little off.

A few weeks after Rachel's funeral, she and Seven suddenly grew towards each other and I watched it happen, the way they were so similar, like they were plants growing towards sunlight, only less healthy. Both attracted to drugs and manic moments, hyper and outrageous, like they only had two versions of themselves: very awake and very asleep. Seven started saying things like, "I'm so glad for Della being around. I still don't trust her," he'd warn me, "but she's good to us. She's not bad, she's just damaged, like me."

When he said that, I was taken aback. Seven didn't seem damaged at all. In fact, he seemed the definition of someone who thrived despite uncertainty.

When we started getting back on our feet, Della took notice, stopped taking care of us and began to sleep a lot longer in the mornings. Seven got her a job at the bar as a bar-back. They spread drugs out on the green coffee table and I felt like the disapproving mother, making big pots of soup and asking them patiently to eat. Doing my homework in the bathroom with earplugs in while they danced around to Pansy Division's "Breaking the Sodomy Law."

They dyed their hair the same shade of green. I shaved my head, vowing to let it grow in natural. Running my hand over my stubbled skull is comforting.

We still have no rules, except that xxxx can't call her here, can't visit. Not in my space. When I see xxxx out I say, *Hello, how are you?* I keep my answers short. I smile politely. I do not look distressed. I give her kisses on both cheeks. She's stopped looking at me like I'm a useless child.

These days Della's eyes are NyQuil pinholes and she moves around the apartment as though it has padded walls. Her journals read like self-help delusions or suicide notes abandoned for sleep. She leaves them open on the coffee table. Seven rolls joints on pages that read *Why can't I change?* Sketches of open skulls and numbered patterns.

She goes to the welfare office and comes back with cartons of cigarettes for the freezer and frozen peas. She is always tired, she is almost always sleeping.

I've cooked and cleaned and bought her favourite movies, magazines, bath salts and fine point markers. Stood at the stove stirring vegan faux-chicken broth and nursed her like her brain had a flu. Suggested therapists. Walks on the mountain. Prozac. Cocaine. Tae Bo. Anything. Something.

I work full-time at the store, take three telephone-survey shifts in the evening. I am rarely home and I am saving up. Seven is working hard on his play, working and typing. We become self-absorbed. Instead of the three of us in bed holding tight and grieving, we turn into three separate bugs spinning yarn of the everyday, toiling and talking to ourselves.

I take her to the YMCA at Parc and Bernard and buy us both memberships. She comes reluctantly. In the locker room our tattoos and scars shout out at the vibrant muscled bodies and the roly-poly seniors in their elastic-waisted jogging pants.

Two old ladies ask Della if she is in the right locker room, mistaking her for a boy. She glares silently and I tell them, *No, she's a girl.* I feel like a traitor for passing, for being the one who has to categorize her complicated gender in this everyday way, just so we can paddle awkwardly in the blue chlorine water.

She says, *See, this was not a good fucking idea.* But I get her into the pool. We both wear bicycle shorts and old Clash T-shirts. She only knows how to doggy-paddle. I can sort of do the breaststroke.

Today is a day off from working at Santé! I'm tired of working for minimum wage and just scraping by. I've been feeling this need to save despite having little to put away after bills are paid. Sealed-up envelopes containing six dollars and seventy-five cents with the amount written in standard ball-point blue on the outside. I slide the disparate amounts under my mattress. String from around vegetables. Jeans with the pockets ripped out of them. Old notes from Jenny written in study hall detailing her sexual exploits. Things are piling up. When the garbage goes out it's all organics, leftover food and things that absolutely have no further purpose. I fold and rinse plastic bags and make flattened stacks under the sink, tied with rubber bands. I'm saving up, I don't know why. I need something to fall back on, I guess.

Last night I was walking home from work holding my hands encased in thin dollar-store black gloves, the kind that could only be cool if you snipped off the tips à la "Lucky Star" era Madonna, but were otherwise useless against the cold. Some asshole on Ste-Catherine Street did the sly walk-by tit rub, the one that's just inadvertent enough not to really have happened. I pictured grabbing him by the throat and slamming his head into the window of the Gap. Violence and sweater vests. I channelled my rage into walking fast, propelled by the excellent new Luscious Jackson CD. By the time I got to Parc and Mont-Royal, I was feeling okay again, all I needed was enough space between my body and someone else's. It is with noted irony that I slipped into the tiny second floor strip club you'd miss if you blinked walking up Parc Avenue with squinty winter eyes. Jenny had left the downtown club for this one closer to home. I had promised her I'd stop in for a drink.

I'd never been into a strip club before. What I had to go on were vaguely romantic eighties daydreams from the movie *Flashdance*. The smell inside the club reminded me of taverns and legion halls in small-town Quebec I'd been to as a kid in the afternoon for sound checks when my father's band was playing. Sitting on the high stools with a flat cola from the taps handed to me by the bartender who took pity on me. Anyone who gave me sugar was an immediate best friend to my six-seven-ten-year-old self, as soda was not usually allowed. I'd twist the straws and pretend it was a cocktail and that I was a rock star waiting for my own sound check. The smell wafted into my nose conjuring that time. The white lights made my heart race. After a curious and squinty-eyed bouncer checked my ID three times and laughed, he said, *Amateur night is tomorrow night.*

"I'm here to see Jewel," I said.

After a good long eyeballing, he pointed me into the club

as if there were many different directions and I might get lost.

It was pretty empty except for a smattering of single men along the sides of the mirrored room, some with dancers on their laps, some with beers, eyes fixed on the stage where a girl in a white bikini top and jean skirt gyrated to Pink Floyd. I didn't expect to feel so out of place. But the only other women were naked and I was in my giant parka, my hair unbrushed, last night's eyeliner fading under my eyes. I felt like a raggedy kindergarten teacher with finger paint on her face. Totally asexual. Like a houseplant.

Out of the darkness came Jenny to hug me. She was unusually tall.

"It's a fucking slow night, but I made some money earlier. Come have a drink." She took my hand and led me to the bar, introduced me to the bartender, Pierre. "I'm glad you came by so I don't have to have another moronic conversation for at least a few minutes."

I told her about how my boss today had instituted a new policy against lunch breaks over fifteen minutes, that Della never left the house, that I was going crazy in this winter hell. Maybe I should work here, save some cash.

Jenny squinted her eyes at me while lighting her smoke, smiling.

"Hmmm. Well, Eve, you could try it out. It'd be fun to have you around."

I could tell by her eyes she thought I was too much of a prude.

"Do you think I could hack it?"

She shrugged. "You'd have to toughen up a bit."

"I am tough."

"You couldn't do that thing that you do, you know."

"What thing?"

"The wide-eyed thing. Like you think everything is so fucking interesting."

"Oh."

"Well, that might work for you, if you wore a schoolgirl uniform or something." She reached out and pushed my scruffy, white blond hair around. "Maybe a ponytail if you grew your hair out."

I bring to mind a scene from a protest a few months earlier when I was the one to call the lawyer's number scrawled on my arm in black pen, backing away from the riot cops because my instinct told me to run run run. I'm always the one checking the stove, making sure the water's not too deep, ascertaining if we should really run across traffic. But Jenny just goes. She acts and determines safety later.

Jenny screamed and yelled and threw her placard on the ground, indignant despite the odds she'd probably be thrown in a cruiser faster than she could say "global capitalism." She threw her disposable camera in an arc over a cop's shoulder to land in my hands, defiant as they dragged her away, pulling her hair and kicking her legs. Not once did she look scared. She even rolled her eyes before the blows hit.

I was five feet away, heart pounding, away from calamity but still terrified; I walked on uneven ground towards the pay phone. Rooting through my messy army green canvas purse for a quarter, I realized then the fundamental difference between us. I observed from the sidelines and she was the show. I thought of things like consequences and she just lived. It depressed me, how cautious I was.

"I'll talk to the manager and see if they need any other girls. You can borrow some of my clothes and," she glanced at my combat boots with the silver stars drawn on the toes, "you'll need some shoes."

An old guy with a facial tic taps her on the shoulder. "Can I get my dance now?"

She turns. Shrugs. "I guess. Wait a few minutes, I'm not done talking."

He smiles nervously, tics a couple of times in a row and goes over to a table, watching the stage show. A girl in a pink one-piece, totally out of time.

Jenny puts her hand on my knee and squeezes. "Things are going to get better, Eve. I can feel it. God, we're not even twenty-one. We're babies!" I've never felt older.

The bartender brings us two tequila shots. Our eyes are lemon slices.

"I feel ancient these days."

"I feel like a newborn." She says, "I have so many plans for us!"

I walk home wondering if I'll take Jenny up on her offer. I daydream that I am red-hot and wanted, wanting. I indulge in my glamorous delusions. On an empty side street I practice pole dancing on an arrêt sign and cut my hand, laughing, hoping no one saw. I picture my bedside table overflowing with fifties and hundreds, my thighs rock hard, smart one-liners tumbling off my lips in quick succession. The girl no one needs to save or walk home late at night.

I go for breakfast the next day with Seven at Pins Pizza. The air in our apartment is stale, the energy charged. I heard him rummaging around at dawn, keeping with these erratic sleeping patterns he's developed recently. I can never guess when he'll be home or keep a plan.

He's already seated in our favourite table by the window, watching the cars race by on Ave du Parc. When I walk in, oversized hot-pink purse threatening to hit other customers as I saunter through the maze of tables, I see that he has two halves of pink grapefruit and six open containers of jam that he was sticking his fingers into.

"I have a hangover. I need to eat more fruit," he says.

"Well, good morning to you, too."

Seven makes me feel normal by comparison. Whatever that is.

It's been nine months since Rachel was killed and he still looks shaky, shifted, permanently like the tattoos on our wrists that spell out her name.

I've never known anyone who died and though Rachel and I weren't that close all the time, I still think about her almost every day. Now it surprises me when a day goes by and I think of her only in the kitchen at night, because I select the mug she gave me with a sixties housewife decal reading *Oops! I guess I forgot to get married!*

I scratch my polished fingernails at breakfast number three. A square waxy photograph of two eggs with sausages, a tin cup of baked beans, and bright tomatoes promises toast and coffee included. I'm definitely eating meat again. The potatoes are indeed God-like, like the menu says.

I watch Seven talking, grateful he isn't Della, but not feeling much more than that. Far away. The closest I'd been to happy since November stomped her heavy boots all over my sense of calm about the world.

"What's wrong with Della these days?"

"She's sad. She doesn't do anything."

"Break up with her." Seven has never had a long-term boyfriend. He says monogamy is for suckers, marriage is a government plot.

I try to think of something to change the subject. "I'm thinking of working at the club with Jenny."

"Oh yeah," Seven says, vaguely interested, not at all surprised. "You're always broke. That might be a good idea, you know. You're not exactly an Amazon but you could work the schoolgirl angle."

I frown. Was cutesy-pedophiliac the only way I could pull off sexy? I look down at my barely there breasts, admit defeat.

"Besides, you're in the right house for it. You know, house of whores and former whores."

"You and Della ..."

"Rachel too."

I knew Seven had turned some tricks when he was a teenager and Della danced one summer when she lived out west, but Rachel?

I raise my eyebrows. "No, that's not true."

"She worked a massage parlour while she was at McGill. Her dad cut her off for being a dyke and that's how she got by."

"Huh, I'd never have guessed. She seemed so, I dunno, unfazed by things."

"Well, she was strong, and you know, very quiet about it. She only ever told me. But I guess now it doesn't matter."

Another thing to add to the list of things that divide me from the friends I love most: all cooler, tougher, bolder. Seven chews the grapefruit rind like a bone and as if he pressed a button in his brain to stop being depressed, he begins bopping his head to pop music on the restaurant radio.

"So, what are you going to do about Sylvia Plath? Where is she anyway? I thought she might come."

"I left her in front of the TV watching *The Price Is Right* and smoking a bowl."

Sometimes I close my eyes at night and put my arms around her. I want things to feel certain. Even when she's pissed me off, even when she cheated and lied, at least I knew what I felt — something always told me I wasn't done with her. Now I'm not so sure.

"I finished the first draft of the play," Seven says. "They're going to let me read it in the afternoon at the club."

"That's awesome, babe."

Seven sips from the white mug of coffee, squinting. "Do you still love her, Eve? The way you used to?"

"This is what love becomes, I think. Sometimes. Hard. Everyone bails." Or perhaps, this is what it's like to fall out of love, I think to myself.

"Why don't you leave her?" Seven asks.

"No, I can't do that." As much as I feel ambivalent, I can't actually picture my life without her.

Often Della will be an enigma, closed, one of those people you just can't read. In the next minute, she becomes so startlingly clear it's as if she's taken a Polaroid of herself and handed it to me. Everything so straightforward and defined.

We sit silently until our plates are cleared, Seven occasionally telling me about the play. Three refills in chipped, white mugs. Seven gets on his cellphone arranging a pick up. My face blushes. Everyone glares at us. He uses it for crisis counselling calls from the hospice and drug deals. Every time he answers it you can tell he doesn't know if he should sound tough or supportive.

"Seven, why don't you use it outside? Everyone's going to think you're ..."

"A hooker? A social worker on call?" He winks.

"No, an asshole."

With that advice, he gets louder and lispier, throwing his red scarf around his neck in a flourish.

"I said eighty for a blow-job, Ramone, you know how hung I am!"

I leave money for the bill on the table laughing and walk out the door, my head tucked into my jacket. The waitress looks annoyed.

16

BASH BACK

What if everything you thought you knew about AIDS *was a lie?* I'm standing in the elevator, reading this poster and I'm thinking some days I wake up thinking everything I think I know is a lie. I'm pretending to be engrossed in the poster to avoid conversation with a potentially chatty stranger. *There is no evidence that* HIV *actually causes* AIDS. The stranger keeps trying to meet my eyes and smiles shyly. I hate talking to strangers. I become frozen in a giant fake grin. All I can say is *um*, or *yeah*, or I lie like a maniac and it comes out so easily that it scares me, like a method actor, these different lives just come flying out of my mouth. As if they are the lives I would've lived if I'd made different choices. *I'm in school, law school*, and they look impressed.

The stranger gets off on the fourth floor and I go up to the ninth where I'm meeting Seven, who's just finishing a meeting for activists who work at AIDS Community Care. It's our weekly post-processing, all-you-can-eat buffet night. Since Rachel died, he's become more active with the ACC, working on his play. It's like the big crazy plans of making time irrelevant have been replaced by pragmatic, positive things.

I'm not thinking too straight. I'm tripping down the sanitary social-service-smelling hallway in my black platform shoes. I watch through the thick glass doors; the meeting looks like it's coming to a close. I can tell because everyone is fidgeting, one person is sleeping and a few questionably committed people are straggling around the coffee machine. Seven is standing at the front of the group in a T-shirt I painted for him that says *Action Equals Life*. He is speaking, loudly, gesturing like a conductor, saying something about harm reduction and I turn on my Walkman and watch him speaking as Cat Power sings. I love this boy. In a way that I've never loved any boy before. In an entirely different way I've ever loved anyone before.

Someone has put a bright red sticker up on the door that says *Bash Back*.

My skin feels like Silly Putty.

Someone pokes me on the shoulder and hands me a flyer. It's a photo of Seven on the front, shirtless, an advertisement for his play. I smile, say, *It looks good*.

When I get home, Della has arranged all of our books in the house by colour and thrown out all the food. I'm really confused. Would normally be angry if I wasn't so strict with making the all-you-can-eat buffet a reality. I don't think I'll be needing food for another day at least.

Tomato has finally come out from hiding and made herself

comfortable on the couch. She looks up at me, meows, as if
to say, *What the fuck is up now?* Gertrude walks over to her
and starts licking her back. They're bonded for life.

"Della, what did you do with the food?"

"I wanted to start things over again. I cleaned the cupboards, put new liners in the drawers. Tomorrow I'll go
shopping."

"What about all the cans of soup and beans? Where did
they go?"

"I gave them to Sun Youth. I brought them over in the
neighbour's red wagon."

She went outside. She talked to the neigbours. She did steal
all my food, but I took this as progress.

I'm relieved to find there are still liquids in the fridge, soda,
soy milk and a carton of orange juice. The milk crate beside
the pet dishes that serves as a makeshift liquor cabinet is full.
I twist open a mickey of Scotch and two-litre bottle of ginger
ale, take two rocks glasses from the newly organized (by
colour) cupboard and pour two shots, fill the rest with fizz.

"We'll start fresh!" she says, gulping down her drink.
"Fresh."

I fall asleep drunk on the couch, listening to her chatter to
the cats about a new system, a new her.

When I wake up dry-eyed and aching a few hours later, Della
is sitting naked in the armchair in front of me, her long legs
spread open, feet dangling over each plush red arm. Her
black and blue hair is wet, curling around her neck, left un-
cut for months longer than usual. My first thought is wow,
she finally took a shower. My second is, she's stunning.

She softly says, "Hey baby," as I get up from the couch, stretch out, staring. I want to take her photograph, wallpaper the room with this image over and over, how beautiful she looks. Pale skin against red chair and the inky lines of her hair.

I grab the Polaroid camera on the green table and snap her image. The flash makes her blink, startled, but her body remains unmoving. I snap another of her outstretched foot. Her wrist. The nape of her neck. I lay them out on the table and watch them develop slowly.

Normally, I'm against nudity. I like to make out clothed, turn off the lights, proceed veiled and shadowed. Nudity is too much of an answer for me, leaving nothing left to discuss or ponder, visualize. If someone takes their clothes off too fast, I usually start thinking about running some errands. But at this moment I feel as though I finally understand the erotic trance mere bodies can cause. I put the camera down, crawl across the room to her, unable to detach my gaze.

I stare up at her, approach softly. She twists her legs around me, clamping her ankles together like a twist-tie. My knees bruising beautifully while her breath rises and falls too many times to count. I don't even tell her to stifle her moans in case we wake up Seven. I'd forgotten what desire feels like.

Afterwards, we smoke cigarettes and drink hot tea on the balcony, our legs resting on the railings, wrapped in blankets, our asses cradled in plastic deck chairs soaked in rain water. The sun is beginning to rise, a pinky glow around us. "Della, how real do you think this death-before-thirty curse is?" Up until this week I hadn't put much real worry into it. But it's fast approaching and this year *had* felt cursed. What if it was really true? I hear Rachel's voice before we passed out on New Year's Eve, *It's the year of the fire rat, a year for natural disasters.*

"My dad thinks it is. He won't stop calling. He wants me to come home and sit in the house until my birthday is over so he can monitor me. He wants my doctor cousin to sit with me and make sure I'm okay."

"I haven't heard any messages from him. When did he call?"

"He calls while you're working mostly."

"Huh. What does your cousin think?"

"He thinks my dad is superstitious and nuts."

"Do you think it's your time?"

"I hope not." Her fingers shake as she puts her cigarette to her lips. "But it's hard to say. My mother, my aunt, my grandmother. All dead at twenty-nine."

"Could be a coincidence. You had a physical last month and everything was fine. You had every blood test under the sun and your doctor said you were perfectly healthy."

Della shrugged. "I know. It's something science can't control. It's beyond us."

"Just remember, all the Tremblays seem to live till ninety-five. You could be more like them. You're not like most women, after all."

"I keep thinking of my mother dying. I see her on her deathbed. I wake up with that image every day."

I don't know what to say to this. I put my hands on her shoulders, kiss her cheek. She doesn't cry. She closes her eyes, puts her cigarette to her lips.

"I have to stop living like I'm about to die. If it's my time, it's my time. Nothing is going to change that."

"Yes, that sounds like a good plan." I say a little prayer right then, opening the balcony door, kicking my slushy shoes on the mat by the cat-food dishes, washing my hands with lavender soap in the kitchen sink to get the smoke smell off. I whisper little prayers to spare her.

17

SEVEN'S PLAY

"Della and Eve," Della says to the girl at the door of the bar. "We should be on the list."

"Yes, oh, here you are." She runs a thin red line through our names and stamps our hands. "The show will begin in about five minutes."

We walk into the bar in a confusing reverse birth, from the afternoon sunlight and into the dungeon, even with all the lights on. The smell of beer and sweat still present from the night before. There are rows of wooden folding chairs placed on the dance floor. I see Melanie and Nicky in the second row. Amanda, the girl Rachel went on the date with the night she died, is setting up the lights. A few of Seven's friends from the ACC are wearing black and setting up the stage area. The floor is covered in chalk outlines of bodies, just like they are in white paint on Ste-Catherine Street. It's a who's who of the queer community. We sit next to Hélène, Della's old friend, who calls me *niblet*. Like baby corn, I guess. My aunt Bev walks in with a long black fake-fur coat and a bright rainbow wool scarf. She sits on a tall stool and waves to us, holding a can of diet soda.

Della goes up to the bar where xxxx is serving, gets us two beers, comes back fast, as if she could sense my discomfort. I tell her she's projecting her guilt. I am sure I've been hiding it well. xxxx is wearing the red dress she once promised me; it strangles her. She looks uncomfortable.

I am nervous for Seven's premiere. Worried that it will be horrible and I'll have to lie. I don't know what to expect, only that he's been rehearsing for weeks now, more sober than he'd been in months, hours of typing at the kitchen table.

The lights go down and Gerard, a well-dressed blond fag in his early thirties I recognize from the ACC, makes an announcement from the stage for everyone to take their seats. He informs everyone this is a work in progress. The room goes black. A Super 8 projector starts rolling and images from the seventies appear, two children in a sandbox, looking up at the camera. It freezes on one face, a girl with pigtails I recognize as Rachel from old photos. A photograph of our wrist tattoos comes into focus, a dedication to Rachel appears. The room goes black again. Seven walks on stage wearing baggy jeans, a tight white T-shirt. He leans against the back wall, lights a cigarette, looks up.

"God, I just want to sleep. I can't sleep at all. I can fuck and I can dance, that should be all I need right? Except I don't have a body. No. Not at all. Huh."

A nineties house song plays, he starts to dance but isn't

coordinated. He stops. The music cuts. Everyone laughs.

"So, I'm in this alley behind the Parc theatre getting my cock sucked by some overeager raver kid I sold some E to. It's time for the Run DMC reunion show and I can't get excited about the show because I'm thinking about Rachel. She's all I can think about."

Photos of Rachel appear behind him.

"I close my eyes and she's stitched to the back of my eyelids." The photos click faster and faster until they blur.

"I don't know if I'm going to bother going in to see the show. We were supposed to go together. It's like I'm all broken up and dissolving, and I'm not too sad about the show 'cause they've gone all born-again Christian anyway. I used to be so into them in Secondary One, me and Rachel both. The only two rap fans in Drummondville, Quebec."

A photo of preteen Rachel and Seven with mullets and Expos T-shirts standing next to a cow clicks on, everyone laughs, while Run DMC plays in the background.

"This is when we ran away from home."

There is a photo of Seven and Rachel and they're dressed like crusty punks, baby faces, standing on the side of a road holding a sign that says *Québec City*.

"We were sixteen."

There are a few more projections of snapshots from their lives together before he moves into the monologue.

"The raver is looking up at me with these pure azure eyes, and he keeps calling me Evan, which is fine. Seven is a strange name, I know. Close enough. I'm wondering why I'm going soft. I fucking hate them. Shut your fucking eyes. He does. I feel a little guilty but I get hard again. My knees are killing me from jumping down off of a fence last night. I felt the crunch and blood rising, but I couldn't stop because I thought the cops were running after me. It turns out my friend Eve was wrong, she'd yelled, *Cop!* but it was only a dog walker. Today I'm paying for it in pain. But I ran and ran and floated away, panting hard against the bathhouse door where I quickly dissolved in the army of bodies, while Della and Eve ran home.

"Eve is my roommate." The lights go down. The film starts again. There I am asleep in bed with Della, her arms around me. "This is them asleep. That's Della, her girlfriend." Then I am riding my bike through the muddy path that cuts the park in two, behind me are the statues on Mont-Royal and the cross. I'm wearing the silver dress from referendum day. I'm smiling because I both love and hate being on camera. The camera slows on my face. I'm smiling like a kid. I barely remember that day. It seems like years ago.

"Anyway, isn't Eve just a fucking sweetheart? A little piece of pie. A cupcake. Usually girls like her drive me nuts, you know, so excitable. Bad tippers, high-pitch gigglers. That's what she was like at first. But it's like every day she wakes up a little more hard core. Anyway, it's really been hard to watch her, like, go through this shit for the first time. I don't know, maybe you lost someone suddenly and you know what I mean. It's like someone handing you a new world and you're not used to the air quality, you don't recognize anything or anyone. Like it is when you're born but there isn't anyone there to teach you how to talk and not swallow rocks and stuff like that. It's like getting punched in the face really slowly. I don't suppose it's all that interesting to you, you probably think I deserve it. I dunno. I guess I'm still sick from what Rachel's mother said to me."

A female actress walks on stage, middle-aged, in respectable dress and church hat and shoes. She says, in French, "*You were supposed to die first. You have the disease God gives to all you sinners. You disgust me. You ruined her. She was such a sweet little girl once.*"

The stage goes black, and Seven reappears.

"I was trying to comfort her, help her clean out her daughter's room. Eve had lost her shit on them, you know, in that self-righteous way you do when you first look up the definition of oppression and realize it applies to you. This woman who used to sing me to sleep and change my diapers, saying stuff like, *You were supposed to die first. It's God's punishment. I can't even look at you.* And for some reason I kept being nice to her because I knew Rachel wouldn't want them to hurt any more than they were. I just kept moving, like it didn't hurt me. I didn't even tell Eve the half of it and I swear some of her hair fell out. I just have to keep going. Rachel would think this whole play was really funny. Hilarious, that I was finally doing something for her. My wrist hurts from my new tattoo. Since her funeral smells have been mixed up, the bagel shop smelled like the ocean and church pews smelled like bales of fresh hay. Me and Eve got the same tattoo, Rachel's name, her date of birth and death. It's opened up a space so we can grieve together. We ducked our skinny frames through the makeshift curtains of Tatouage Iris on Ontario, held our pink raised skin together.

"Anyway, after I get off with the raver kid, I walk back out onto the street. Gerard rides up on his blue bike like it's any ordinary Parc Avenue night, the basket of his bike filled with condoms and safer sex info pamphlets. Gerard is tireless. He launches into some fucking New Age monologue about having been shopping for his inner child. He grabs my shoulder and looks into my eyes and says something about why can't he just let himself be happy, you know life is short, and he shouldn't be afraid to love and let go and why can't he get over his nasty childhood already since he's thirty-three. Gerard always tries to get me to fuck him. I feel like, despite his constant crusade for safer sex and harm reduction, he really just wants to hurry up and get AIDS so he can write a bestselling memoir. He's still talking. For one split second he forgets that he's a Leo and the world revolves entirely around him and looks at me like he's only just now realized I'm there.

"'How are you, Seven?' Sometimes he talks just like a social worker, soft lilts, like he knows he's talking to someone whose life is shit or soon to be shit. Mixed with the pity he feels is this sick fascination with the glamour that comes out when he's drunk and trying to stick his tongue in my mouth. He's looking at me like he can't wait to hear something juicy. Real. Hard."

Words come up on the screen behind him. They read, *Sorry Gerard*. Gerard laughs from the sidelines, says, *Busted*.

"So I give it away. Why not? I tell him, in my best deadpan lisp, that Rachel is dead. He looks shocked. She never liked him anyway, calling him an earnest yuppie fag who always bums cigarettes even though he's loaded. His eyes widen and then he looks at me like I'm seven years old and I've got leukemia and I'm about to fall over. And he says, over and over, with this impetuous grip-slash-hug, that he's so sorry and, 'Are you okay? Are you okay? You can't be okay. What can I do?'

"'Sure, Gerard, sure.' I walk away while he is still talking. Grief gives you this incredible gift of being able to be an asshole without consequences. Don't let my bravado fool you, my body has begun its own twitchy muscular apocalypse that starts in my neck and ends in my numb little toe. I'm wearing three layers of Rachel's shirts, a wife beater under a *Rock for Choice* T-shirt under a flannel plaid button-down. I'm smoking all of her leftover cigarettes. Gerard would say I'm experiencing Survivor Guilt. He would have a book I could read. So, by 4:00 a.m. I am making out with another kid in the bus shelter on Bernard. It's cold and it's meaning-less, we are not compatible kissers anyway. I'm not sure why I stay there as long as I do. I'm running my tongue over misplaced thoughts and memories. I would trade in my brain for fourteen cents and a pack of cigarettes right now. This is no sob story. No climb every mountain. No Cokes for the whole world. I flash on our high-school prom, the way she said, 'Seven, I have to tell you, I have a crush on Christine Martindale. Do you think I'm going to go to hell?' From that uncertain little kid to the way she grew up to stare at anyone, never hiding her longing. Ink like blood on flat white pages. The ambition of a herd of stampeding animals, the best wit, the hardest heart.

"Eve brings home Della, who grunts at me inaudibly when she comes into the kitchen to get water. She hands me a warm pile of red and blue gummy worms and smiles. 'You're going to be okay, Seven. I know it.' There is something very reassuring about this, sometimes the way Della speaks like she's an old man on top of a mountain dispensing necessary truths to the clueless, even if I know enough not to believe everything that comes out of her mouth. I watch Eve move around the kitchen, hair all tousled, armpit hair jutting out from her tiny arms, a simple black cotton mini-dress she's been wearing since the funeral. I want to ask her what to do but know she won't likely have a lot of insight. Eve has never known anyone who's died, she's like this adorable raucous baby chick devastated by this, but she's able to eat and stand still. Here I am, I've been to dozens of funerals and this feels like the hardest task I've ever had to complete. How come she's not falling apart? When was the last time I slept? All I can think to write is, *I can and have lived with almost anything but I can't be alone with this.*"

The film shows Della, Seven and me on the couch. We do not smile. It's a photo Rachel took on the morning of January 1, 1996. We look like we knew what was about to come.

The stage goes black and the room is so quiet we can hear Seven exhaling as he walks off the stage.

When the lights come up, there is a solid offering of applause and some hollers. Seven walks back and takes a bow and I try to catch his eye, but I don't. Della puts a smoke behind her ear and pulls on her coat. I look at Aunt Bev and there are tears in her eyes and she's holding her hand to her heart. I am envious of her outpouring of emotion as I can't seem to demonstrate exactly how Seven's play moved me. I smile at her warmly, and she walks towards me with open arms.

We go across the street to a café and share pieces of cake and hot chocolate. Della looks relaxed for the first time in months. Seven holds my hand under the table. We listen to Aunt Bev talk about religion and politics, every once in a while she links it back to Seven's play. "You must be so proud, Seven. You should really be so proud."

Seven stares at Bev, who stares back just as intently.

"Uh, thanks."

18

VEGAN SOUP
OF THE DAY

The Santé! corporation has decided to open café franchises in each of their stores. After weeks of enduring sawdusty air and protruding nails, we have a new corner with café tables and chairs and a coffee bar with stools, a simple menu with sandwiches and soup. I find sprouts in the curve of my rolled-up pant legs. There are new staff members that speak like automatons and don't like gays. "She's trying to get rid of all the dykes," Melanie informs me.

"Are you paranoid or something?"

Later when my boss catches me kissing Della outside the store, she pulls me aside to say I should be more discreet, to think about how we reflect the store. Considering how many times I've caught my boss in the dry goods aisle dry humping her husband in full view of Mrs. Edelson, our most regular client, I realize Melanie's right.

I dream about rinsing sprouts at night. I dread going to work and feel absorbed in work politics when I'm there, thinking about it far too much after I leave. With this new café development, the really deliberate shoppers tend to lounge even more slowly while they sip herbal tea and write out their dietary needs on thick slabs of recycled napkins, parking their bony butts on chairs for hours, thumbing through free magazines.

I stand at the counter, restocking straws and shaking the raw sugar bowl. I tear off a piece of bread to throw in the bowl, make sure the sugar doesn't clump. I doodle caricatures of our regular customers, squiggling wrinkles into foreheads, betraying them as they are, shaky and pale, depressed and listless. I draw mountains of nutritional supplements.

A girl with red hair walks in, ringing the new wind chimes, overshadowed by her enormous hiking backpack. She wears an unfortunate socks-and-sandals combo, and a sweat line crosses her brow. She stands, staring at the new chalkboard menu behind our heads at the cash. She stands there for a few minutes, I nod, signalling I'm paying attention to her. She smiles, sings along with the Ani DiFranco the new automaton has taken to playing on repeat. None of us are pretty girls, indeed. I turn some of the nutritional supplements I'm sketching into bombs.

Mel, who is restocking the coffee bean wall looks at me, rolling her beautifully and excessively made-up eyes, mouthing, *She's a nightmare.*

"Do you know what you want?"

"Um, is the soup vegan?"

The sign says Vegan Soup of the Day.

"Yes."

Tap tap tap, red pen on the side of the counter. The more I smile, the more she smiles. Eventually one of us is going to be all tonsil and tiny eye sockets. She has sweet little red braids tied in rainbow ribbon. Political buttons on the overflowing backpack. *Lower Tuition Fees. This is What a Bisexual Looks Like. Free East Timor.* She bothers me.

She puts a pencil in her mouth. The pencil scrapes against her teeth, a virile little pixie and beaver hybrid. She looks so innocent. She pushes her sleeve up and reveals a tattoo of a faerie. It's pretty, but it makes me hate her. I'm too tired.

My right calf erupts in tiny splints of pain. Like the faerie has jumped off her wrist and begun devilishly gnawing on my leg. I can hear it giggle. Ani DiFranco warbles and hiccups, breathless over the speakers, and the girl sings along, off tune.

I haven't come down from the drugs I took last night.

That might make a difference here.

All three of us went out dancing wearing tutus and crazy wigs. We were celebrating the success of Seven's play. It felt like the times things were good, like we were remembering a time before Rachel died, even though things were never this good then, because they were just normal, and ordinary is never the kind of good you remember. I looked at Della and I didn't feel any anger for cheating, any suspicion. I memorized their faces. It's like we couldn't have appreciated a night like this before. We drank red and purple cocktails and they did lines of coke off the insides of my wrists and we exclaimed our love for each other over loud beats of appreciation. I tried a little bump off a key in the bathroom and didn't feel any different at all. Except I realized later how fast I was talking.

I expected to feel intoxicated, but instead I felt more acutely sober than I ever had before. Nothing like pot or drinking, just this odd new angle. We kept picking up Seven's cellphone pretending to be calling our stockbrokers. It was juvenile and glittery and much needed. Seven and Della dropped acid with our friend Hélène at last call and I decided to be good, go home, make sure I could make it to work at 10:00 a.m.

We all hugged goodbye in a circle. It felt like the best part of high school, only happily, we were no longer in high school.

After collecting my jacket from coat check I went back in to get my key from Seven's pocket. I caught a glimpse of Della and Seven, dancing like fools. I smiled to myself goofily, aware that things felt okay again, even if just for a moment. Whatever happened in the future, there was now a permanence among Seven, Della and me that couldn't be broken. Beyond Della and me as a couple, or the three of us as roommates, as individuals we felt linked.

Leaving the bar, I noticed xxxx in the line for coat check with Isabelle. I walked right by them. It's been long enough that we can pretend to be strangers.

I ran my hands over my apron, a soothing lavender colour embroidered with a smiling cow, featuring sloppy embroidered text that reads *A Burger Stops a Beating Heart*. It's covered in cranberry-spelt muffin mix. My shirt is half untucked. My hair is escaping a formerly tight ponytail.

"Um, what exactly is in the tofu carrot mushroom miso stew?"

"Tofu, carrots, mushrooms, in a miso sauce."

"Yeah, I mean, like, what are all the ingredients ..."

I prattle off a list of words, half of which I make up for ease of interaction. She's going to be allergic to something, I can tell.

"Oh, red peppers make me sleepy. I'm allergic, I think."

My left thumb is making a distinct sweat print on the pad of paper. I feel really faint. I can't remember when I last ate something. The door jingles with those godawful New Age charms that are supposed to fill the room with calm. My heart races. My nose feels raw from the coke and I feel the chemical drips down the back of my throat returning. I make a mental note to never do it again. I can't believe I did it in the first place. So eighties.

Seven is suddenly standing behind me, hands on my hips.

"Eve, I need to talk to you ..."

I half-turn my head, feel my chin against his chest. "Seven, I hafta take this order ... you're not supposed to be behind the counter." I look around for my boss. Melanie shouts, "She's on lunch! Don't worry."

"You're not here to fuck with me 'cause you're still cracked out are ya?" Did I say that out loud? Too loud? Volume is not on my side today. Girl in red braids smiles so hard her mouth cracks into the rest of her face. I see stars around her head. Melanie looks at me from across the room and mouths, *Everything okay?*

Braid girl looks poised to speak, then turns back to scan the menu with a red nail. "I don't know ... hmmm ..."

"Eve ..."

Ani DiFranco is going on about both hands.

"Why not try the soup and sandwich combo?"

"Eve!"

"I can't have wheat ..."

"Eve *hostie*!!"

"Excuse me ... Drama Queen needs me for a sec." I try to give her a sympathetic eyebrow raise, like, you know how it is, when your crackhead best friend has a drug-induced breakdown at your job. She half-smiles.

His lip is covered in blood. Chewing, I surmise. I reach up with my apron to dab his face and he backs away. "It's okay, it's okay. It's just ..."

He says okay five times or more, convincing me with each syllable how un-okay he is. I walk him behind the counter, sit him on a plastic bucket of coffee beans, put my hand against his pale face. "Do you need a sandwhich? Some water? Whatever it is, it's okay."

Seven doesn't look assured by my practised soothing voice. "It's Della, she stayed at Hélène's last night ..."

"Yeah, I told them to crash there so they wouldn't keep me up all night with their acid bullshit."

"So, like, this is hard to say, I'm just going to have to say it, um ..."

"Why are you sounding so retarded? Did they fuck or something? It's not a big deal if they did, you know. I'm cool about that kind of thing now, you know, no rules."

"Della, I can't find her! No one can! Hélène's apartment burned down this morning ... some wiring problem they think, the police think that she might have been in the building. Hélène escaped, and she thinks that Della might have gone out exploring after she fell asleep, but she was so high, she can't really remember. And no one can find Della. Hélène's looked everywhere!"

"Lentil soup, excuse me, I'll have the lentil soup." Braid girl chimes in loudly from a few feet away.

"That's impossible! That would be too much of a big joke with the before-thirty curse. I mean, her birthday is this Sunday. That's just too ridiculous." I produce a sharp and gasping alien-like laugh.

Seven stands up from the coffee pail and tries to hug me. "I don't know what to do, like, where would she be? I went home. She's not there. I went by the diner, the park, the café ... nothing!" He tells me that he even called xxxx.

"She's probably wandering around, still tripping out. You know, she'll talk to anyone. Maybe she's home by now." I pick up the batter-stained phone and dial home. It rings and rings.

"The police say the fire is totally out now and they haven't found a body," Seven says hopefully.

A body?

"Excuse me ... why aren't you answering me? I told you I would like the —"

I turn around sharply and hurl the phone at the braid girl's face. She blocks it with her hands but it still knocks her over.

I walk towards the new, sparkling industrial fridge. Feel its cool metal face. A body?

Black. Stars. Mercury tongue.

19

THE SIZE OF
THIS PROVINCE

I come to as the braid girl is screaming, "Why'd she do that, why?" Mel holds a can of Blue Sky cola to her face and tries to calm her. Seven is resting me in his arms in front of the freezer. "You haven't been out for long, just like ten seconds." He answers his phone.

"Where are you????" He pauses for a second, listening, while I concentrate on not throwing up. He drops the phone. "Della's okay, she's okay, she's in the mental hospital." He picks it up again and asks her for details. "We'll be right there ... don't let them give you shock treatments or anything."

"The mental hospital?" I breathe. I've never been so happy to hear that someone I love is in the bin. Locked up. Safe. Weird.

"She said she took off her shirt at the Quatres Sous grocery store as a political statement and now the doctors are afraid of women's power and we have to go break her out."

What? Della was not one of those shirtless hippie lesbians. This sounded very weird.

Once I can stand, my boss yells at me to get the hell out of the store before she calls the police. It seems so absurd when the cold air outside hits me that one laugh escapes my lips. Then another. Like a cough. Then it's uncontrollable. I'm hiccup-laughing, guts aching, and Seven gives up trying to calm me, choosing instead to join in. We hail a cab and say, *The Montreal General! The Psych Ward!* Snot and tears drip down our faces, hysterical giggles escaping with each breath out.

We aren't allowed to see her. We remain out of hope. We're not family. I laugh at that. Her dad leaves his hometown once a year, if that. Her mother is dead and I have no idea how to find her brother, who does not appear to be listed in any phone book in Quebec. We could also be barred because we are suspiciously crazy looking and Seven's shirt says *That's Mr. Faggot to you.* We sit in the waiting room for hours, exhausted, lips chewed like the edge of a worried paper coffee cup. We play I Spy, Truth or Dare, chewing insipid, stale corn chips; we press E9 instead of E8, the coveted licorice nibs. I have too much time to panic about losing my job. *It's retail, you'll get another one in a second*, Seven assures me.

Pushing through the double doors to the waiting room, xxxx bursts in like that kind of gum with liquid in the middle, squirting her command all over the room. She's breathless, long curly hair flipped dramatically. I hadn't thought to call her — how did she know?

"Cherie, where is she?! A doctor called me and told me she listed me as her next of kin?"

I cast my eyes downward and see that my right hand is pointing her towards the nursing station like a tour guide, a polite airline stewardess. When xxxx tosses her hair towards the bitchy nurse at the counter, Mrs. Glare-at-the-punk-kids turns into a completely different person; her posture shifts. I can tell she thinks xxxx deserves respect. They speak in fast French. xxxx fills out some forms and gets led in right away.

I exhale a sigh the size of this province.

Seven's eyes are so wide, his shoulders in a permanent shrug of, *What the fuck?*

I pull my red and black notebook, the kind you find at Warsaw's for two bucks, out of my backpack. I squeeze Seven's hand, admire the chipped silver polish on his nails. His hands are shaking. I try to hold them still in mine.

I start writing with, *In this liminal space, we are marking the hospital chairs with dirt-filled, creased spiral marks from the pads of our fingers.*

I end with: *I'm no longer keeping score.*

I cuddle up to Seven, click on my Walkman. "Cold Cold Hearts" plays. I sleep so soundly even while waiting. I'm just really used to waiting. I feel Seven get up a few times, sit back down. Drape his jacket over my lap. I have a ridiculous dream with an obvious metaphor about Della being on a life raft unravelling and I'm made of fire but somehow still alive.

I wake up to the click of my Walkman and his persistent tapping on my shoulder. His eyes are wider than they have been all day, he no longer has any irises, just pupil.

There's a woman in a black dress, fur coat draped over one arm, standing at the desk yelling at the nurse, "I want to see my daughter! Where is my fucking daughter? Her name is

Della Tremblay." She speaks to the nurse like she's a total idiot.

Seven and I stare at each other and then at the woman, incredulous. I stand up, walk towards her, chest pumped out, hands palms up, curled like question marks.

"That can't be possible, Della's mother is dead."

"Oh, I'm perfectly alive, who the hell are you?"

"I'm Eve. I'm her girlfriend!"

The woman snorts. "Sure. Sure you are." She flits her hands around nervously like I'm a mosquito gunning for her drink.

"Listen, a doctor called me. I'm here to see my daughter and I demand to be let in immediately!"

As if on cue xxxx comes through the heavy locked doors that buzz when opened.

"Oh thank God, Katherine! You're here taking care of things," says the woman. "She's really done it to herself this time, eh?" As if Della had got herself an ugly tattoo or a bad haircut.

Katherine embraces the woman. They hug like sisters. I'm still standing there, gutted. I feel my skin slipping away in careful fillets. Bottle rocket diffused. This is Della's "dead" mother. Her reason for being sad, not keeping jobs, her reason to worry about dying before Sunday. This was her reason for cheating on me? This bitch in a fur coat ignoring me? The reality and scope of betrayal, the layers and layers of lies, feel almost too thick to even comprehend.

I let out, "Ha. Huh. Fuck."

Katherine looks at me, confused. "What's wrong, Eve? Haven't you met Della's mother before? Mrs. Tremblay, this is Eve. Eve, Mrs. Tremblay."

"It's Ms. Johnson now, I've changed it back."

I don't take her hand. They don't seem to notice, just walk through the doors closed to me.

"Let's get out of here," I hear Seven say from several miles away. "Let's go get a drink."

"Yes, let's." I take his small clammy hand in mine and we walk outside. The cold air hits me like a punch of new ideas.

Isabelle arrives breathless just as we get a few metres from the hospital doors.

Seven takes my hand. I feel ridiculous.

Isabelle opens the doors to the hospital as I am contemplating where to go. "Katherine told me that Della wants to see you, Eve. She's asking for you. Where are you going?"

"Yeah?" I say, inhaling. "Well, I've got to be somewhere."

She pauses, looks me in the eye, almost as if to say, *Run run run*.

"Yeah, okay. I'll tell her."

"Listen, I'm going to pack her shit and leave it in the front hall. Just have Katherine come pick it up some time, okay?"

Katherine comes out just as Isabelle nods. Lights a cigarette. "Eve, you're not leaving?" She sounds panicked.

I feel an outer-body sense of peace, complete calm. "I'm getting out of here. I'll see you later, Katherine."

I keep Seven's hand in mine, lace my fingers through his like we're grade-school pals. I hear Katherine saying, "What the fuck? She can't leave. What the hell? Della asked for her! How can she just go?"

"Let's go split a pitcher at the Bifteque and stare at the straight boys," I suggest.

We walk down the paved incline, and with each icy step I'm decidedly changed, just like that day on the mountain where Della held my hand. Things are just as clear, clearer even. My heart beats strong and purposefully, no longer a panic-driven metronome. Della is a story I will tell to reference my last stretch of adolescence. Those years I dated a fiction. She's locked up and I am anywhere I choose to be.

Seven and I walk away like a duo in the last panel of a comic book, fading from bright colours to black and white. I fasten an invisible cape around my neck, lean into Seven's shoulder. I feel soft and furious.

ACKNOWLEDGEMENTS

Many thanks for Samantha Haywood at the Transatlantic Literary Agency for her endless support and enthusiasm for my work; Marc Côté and Angel Guerra and everyone at Cormorant Books, the Ontario Arts Council for financial support through the Works-in-Progress and Writers' Reserve programs. Thank you to Sumach Press, Broken Pencil Magazine, Descant Quarterly and Cormorant Books for recommending the book for writers' reserve grants. For reading the earliest drafts, I am indebted to Marnie Woodrow, Gavin Downie, Jess Carfagninni, Mariko Tamaki, Trish Salah, Tara-Michelle Ziniuk and Chloe Brushwood-Rose for their editorial insight and opinions. Thank you Liz Vanderkleyn for copy-editing the first draft, and Lisa Foad, Will Scott, and Jennifer Scott for reading the late drafts. Many thanks to Megan Richards for helping me with details around the referendum, setting the scene, for stealing some important memories. Thank you to Suzy Malik for feeding me both insight and dinner during three crucial years writing this book. Thanks to Joe Pert, Ange Holmes, Jenn Scott and Will Scott for allowing me to poach little lines from their lives and to listen to my endless drafts. I am forever grateful for all the metaphors and witticisms I plucked from conversations and inserted into the lives of my characters. Thank you Kristyn Dunnion and Emily Shultz.

For research purposes I consulted *Breaking Point — Quebec/ Canada, the 1995 Referendum* (CBC/Bayard Books Canada, 2005) written by Mario Cardinal and translated by Ferdinanda Van Gennip, with Mark Stout.